11 - 15

THE BLOODY QUARTER

A Western Story

Other Five Star Titles
by Les Savage, Jr.:

Fire Dance at Spider Rock
Medicine Wheel
Coffin Gap
Phantoms in the Night

THE BLOODY QUARTER

A Western Story

LES SAVAGE, JR.

Five Star
Unity, Maine

An earlier version of this story appeared in somewhat different form as "Drink to a Lobo's Guns" in *Lariat Story Magazine* (9/46). Copyright © 1946 by Real Adventures Publishing Co. Copyright © 1950 by Les Savage, Jr. Copyright © renewed 1974, 1978 by Marian R. Savage.

Five Star Western Series
Published in conjunction with Golden West Literary Agency.

Cover photograph by Johnny D. Boggs

September 1999

Standard Print Hardcover Edition.

First Edition

Five Star Standard Print Western Series.

The text of this edition is unabridged.

Set in 11 pt. Plantin by Minnie B. Raven.

Printed in the United States on permanent paper.

Library of Congress Cataloging-in-Publication Data

Savage, Les.
    The bloody quarter : a western story / by Les Savage, Jr.
    — 1st. ed.
        p. cm.
    "Five Star western" — T.p. verso.
    ISBN 0-7862-1581-X (hc : alk. paper)
    I. Title.
PS3569.A826B58   1999
    813′.54—dc21   99-35657

THE BLOODY QUARTER

Chapter One

Paul Hagar was in the saddle before dawn, riding out First Street where it paralleled the Union Pacific tracks. A train coming into Laramie hooted mournfully in the distance, and its headlight was a glaring Cyclop's eye splitting the night. For three hours he bucked the broken country north of town. The soupy dawn mists began steaming from the ground, and then a rising sun caught him pulling into the compound of the Aspen Creek way station. Wood smoke mingled its bittersweet tang with the strong smell of coffee. The station-keeper shambled from the door, scratching sleepily at a mop of straw-colored hair. Hagar asked for coffee, and the man turned to shout back into the building.

"Two coffees out here, Len." Then he turned sleep-puffed eyes back to the end of the rolled newspaper sticking from one of Hagar's saddlebags. "May Thirtieth, Eighteen Eighty-Six," he mused. "How'n hell did you get this morning's *Eagle* so early? It won't even hit the Laramie streets till eight."

Hagar stepped off the horse. "Maybe I know the editor."

Suspicion took the sleep from the man's eyes. "Heading north. War Bonnet's up that way. Don't tell me the government's finally opened the land for filing up there."

Hagar moved away from the rank smell of his heated horse, wanting to let her cool before he watered the animal. "I wouldn't know."

"Damn you," the man said with amiable anger. "You wouldn't be on the road with that paper for any other

7

reason. All the legal printing in these counties is done at Laramie. They won't even get the word in War Bonnet till the Laramie stage hits there this evening. That must mean the Land Office opens tomorrow."

Hagar grinned ruefully, realizing it was no use trying to hide it. "Eight o'clock tomorrow evening the rush starts."

"That's better," the man said. "You know I can't do you any harm, far as filing goes. I'm stuck here. I wouldn't want no part of it, anyway. I've seen them rushes. They'll be lined up for blocks, soon as the news breaks in War Bonnet. Waiting all night. Fighting like cats and dogs." The boy came with two cups of coffee, and the station-keeper took one. "Hear that, Len? The Laramie land is being opened tomorrow. This man wants to be the first in line."

With a gap-toothed grin, the kid handed over the coffee, settling a close look on Hagar's face. It was a face that tended to gauntness, a habitual wariness filling it with a brooding quality. The jaws were hard and the cheekbones high, molding into steady gray eyes that were crow-tracked at the tips from sun and wind and a constant study of life. The Roman nose had been broken in a barroom fight long ago and had healed crookedly, adding to the hawkish aspect of the face.

"You don't look like no homesteader," the kid said.

"Maybe he's a speculator," the station-keeper chuckled, making a slurping sound with his coffee. "You won't make no money out of that grassland, friend. It's too hard for cattle to reach . . . in them mountains."

"There's always some kind of deal," Hagar said, draining the cup in long gulps. When he was finished, he handed it back, along with a nickel, and turned to lead his hammerheaded buckskin to the water butt. He heard the drum of hoofs before he reached the water, but paid little attention, thinking it was one of the stage horses running a corral fence. Then it began to shake the ground, and he turned to see a long-legged bay coming down the road at a hard gallop. He had an instantaneous impression of its rider, young, expensively dressed, with a wisp of a mustache and arrogant eyes. Hardly checking his stride, the man wheeled the bay in toward the water butt, shouldering against Hagar's horse. The buckskin danced aside to regain her footing, almost knocking Hagar over. Hagar ducked under his horse's neck and dragged the bay's bit, jerking it away from the trough.

"Didn't you ever learn to wait in line?" he asked angrily.

The man jerked on his reins, trying to yank the bit free of Hagar's grip. "Let go, damn you, I'm in a hurry!"

"If you'd asked, I'd have been glad to give you a drink," Hagar said thinly. "Right now I think you'd better get away and let my horse back where she was."

"Damn you!" The man shook loose a quirt looped about his right wrist and swung it hard.

Hagar released the bit to throw up his arm. The quirt lashed across his wrist instead of his face. Its biting pain filled him with hot anger. He caught the man's arm before he could pull it back, putting his whole weight on it. He saw the look of startled surprise on the man's face as he was pulled out of the saddle.

It brought him down onto Hagar and knocked Hagar to the ground with him. Hagar rolled out from under and came to his hands and knees. Instead of trying to rise, the rider rolled over and went for his gun. Hagar lunged to his feet, reaching him as the gun freed leather. He lashed out a boot to kick the six-shooter out of the man's hand as it went off.

Face twisted with pain, the man rolled over and threw himself at Hagar from hands and knees. Hagar danced back from the charge till the man was on his feet and rushing forward completely off balance. Then Hagar stopped, set himself, and let the man run right into his first blow. It hit him in the belly. He doubled over Hagar's fist like an empty sack.

Hagar pulled his fist back and hit the man in the face before he could fall. The blow straightened him and knocked him backward so hard he smashed into the wall of the stage station. He hung there for a moment, pain making a foolish mask of his face. Then he slid to a sitting position against the logs.

The towheaded kid stood by the station door holding Hagar's coffee cup, gaping at him. "Jee-hoshaphat," he breathed.

Hagar towered over the fallen man, panting heavily. "Want to try again?" he asked.

The man held his arms hugged around his belly, his face sick and white. He stared up at Hagar with hate and pain in his squinted eyes. He tried to rise, but his face twisted, and he sank back down with a retching sound. Hagar turned away and went to pick up the gun. He jacked the shells out of the fancy presentation Colt with the gold-chased grips, dropped them into his coat pocket, then threw the gun at the man's feet.

"Next time," he said, "maybe you'll be polite."

The man made another effort to rise. Once on his feet, he leaned against the wall, breathing shallowly. Finally he stooped to pick up his gun and jam it into his holster. It made him dizzy, and he had to catch at the wall again. At last, he swept Hagar with hate-filled eyes, then let them swing on around to the station-keeper. "You'll be hearing from Garland about this, Hackett."

Apprehension close to fear darkened the station-keeper's face. "Now wait a minute, Carter," he said, holding out a protesting hand. "I didn't have anything to do with. . . ."

"I said you'd be hearing from Garland." The words left the man in a waspish voice. He turned back to Hagar, a tremor of rage running through his words. "And so will you!"

He then wheeled and swung aboard the bay so hard it started to rear. He raked it brutally with the spurs, and the beast bolted, racing away in a cloud of dust. Hagar spat the grit from between his teeth, staring after the man. The whole thing had an unreal quality now. He felt a strange surprise that it should be over, a feeling that it had actually never happened. Violence was like that. Sweeping in without reason, over as swiftly as it had started.

"You shouldn't have done that," Hackett said. "That's Carter John. That's Ed Garland's nephew."

"Nobody takes a quirt to me," Hagar said.

The kid gaped at him. "Don't you know who Ed Garland is?"

"The biggest man in Wyoming," Hagar said. "I know. I wouldn't even let *him* quirt me."

In his rage, Carter John had forgotten the quirt. Hagar moved over to the water butt and stooped to pick it up. The braided butt had a gold head engraved with an E Bar G.

"That's Ed Garland's own quirt," the gap-toothed boy said. There was awe in his voice. "I seen him carrying it in Laramie."

"Wonder what Carter John was doin' with it," Hackett muttered. Then he looked up the road. "For that matter, I wonder why the hell he was heading north in such a scramble."

Hagar idly looped the quirt and stuffed it in the top of his boot, staring after Carter John, too. "Yes," he murmured, "I wonder."

★ ★ ★ ★ ★

Beyond the Aspen Creek station the Laramie Plains rose into the first mountains. Through the forenoon and early afternoon Hagar followed the road over windswept ridges and into shadow-filled cañons, the penetrating scent of pine always with him, the timber-shrouded slopes billowing up toward a cloudless sky. More than once, in the high parks, he sighted cattle with Ed Garland's E Bar G on their flanks, and it kept his mind on Carter John. He followed the Fetterman Cutoff through Eagle's Nest Gap. The Cheyenne and Black Hills Stage kept another way station in the gap, and he stopped there to water his horse again and to eat. From the hostler he learned that Carter John had passed through an hour earlier, pushing a tiring horse hard.

It bothered Hagar. He kept wanting to connect it with the opening of the government land around War Bonnet. Yet he knew that was foolish. The nephew of a man Ed Garland's size wouldn't go to so much trouble to speculate on such a low level. The most a man could hope to gain out of it was a few hundred dollars. Hagar shrugged, climbing back onto his horse. Why worry about it? There were probably a hundred more such riders on the road behind him now, in the saddle as soon as the *Eagle* hit the streets of Laramie with news of the opening. The stage would be loaded down with men hoping to file—either to homestead or to speculate. He'd have to push hard himself, if he meant to stay ahead of them.

He rode the day out, till the sun was well down in the west, with purple shadows casting their insubstantial skeins over the steeply pitched slopes. The wind from the north was blowing harder, and the buckskin was tiring. Hagar was taking it easy, trying to give her a breather for the last push into War Bonnet. He knew the town could not be much farther now. He was picking his way slowly through a stand of blue spruce, crowning one of the ridges, when the shots came.

They made a double whiplash, spooking his weary buckskin. The echoes seemed to crash and reverberate for long seconds through the endless corridors of the hills before shivering into silence.

Hagar had his Winchester out of its boot and a shell jacked into the firing chamber, before those echoes were dead, and was pulling the skittish horse into the dubious cover of timber siding the road. He sat there, holding a tight rein on the fiddling horse. As he realized how far off the shots had been, a wry smile tilted his lips. He had pulled the Winchester without thought. What a strange groove the habits of a lifetime had hammered him into.

Carefully he worked the buckskin deeper into the timber, dropping off the ridge so that he would not be skylighted, yet keeping near its summit so he would have the advantage of height. The road shelved down into a narrow valley beneath him, and it was hard to define much in the black shadows at the bottom. Then there was faint motion on the opposite ridge, and Hagar felt habituated reaction run through him again, lifting his rifle. A horseman was silhouetted on the crest for a moment, over there. He seemed to take a look back into the valley. Then he dropped off on the other side and disappeared.

Hagar sat there for another space, still reluctant to expose himself. Finally he started to move out. It was then that he caught sight of the horse in the valley. It moved into the treacherous half light between the mats of black shadow. It was running hard, evidently spooked by the shots, and its saddle was empty. Just before the next shadows swallowed it, Hagar recognized the animal. It was the blooded bay that Carter John had ridden.

When the horse had disappeared, he moved cautiously across the road and into the timber beyond, working down toward the bottom on the steep slopes rather than the road. Finally he reached level ground and found the bay's tracks, plainly cut into red sandstone washings from the hills. The valley floor was a tangle of greasewood and sagebrush, with early bluebells spreading their transient beauty in sheltered corners. He backtracked along the bay's trail through the woodland till he reached the open space, a little park bordered by ragged lodgepole pine and carpeted with browning grass.

A magpie scolded sleepily as Hagar dismounted. The wind was soft as a lover's sigh through the treetops. The man lay on his back with a faintly bewildered look on his face. Hagar saw where the two bullets had torn murderously through Carter John's chest. They wouldn't have made that much mess going in. He had been shot in the back.

Hagar knew a moment's compassion for the man. Their fight, their intense anger of a few hours ago held little significance now. Hagar felt the thread of shock, perhaps of awe, that always ran through him at sight of a human life snuffed out. He had heard this man's voice, had seen him torn by anger and pain, had met the solid resistance of his animate body. And now all of it was gone. It gave Hagar an empty feeling at the pit of his stomach.

Staring bleakly down at the corpse, he realized he could not take the body into War Bonnet. There was little chance of finding the bay at night. It was probably miles away by now. His own horse was too played out to carry double. The best he could do was cover the man and report the killing. He put enough rocks and brush on Carter John to keep the wolves off, and then mounted again and sought the road through a twilight that was rapidly thickening into night.

14

Chapter Two

When in 1886 the Fremont, Elkhorn, and Missouri Valley Railway announced its intent of extending a line westward from Chadron, Nebraska up the Platte River, men of foresight formed the Pioneer Townsite Company and established a permanent site for the town some eight miles east of old Fort Fetterman. Streets were laid out at the very intersection of the Bozeman and Texas Trails, and, before the first passenger train arrived, the first lot sold for seven hundred and ninety dollars. The new town was named War Bonnet.

War Bonnet sprawled out across the flats of a surprise valley deep in the Laramie Mountains. It was as if nature had tired of the endless undulation of ridges and peaks and had scooped a Gargantuan handful of earth out from their midst, leaving a bold slice that ran for ten miles between steep parallel ridges and then boxed off right against the backbone of the mother mountains. The one long street of the town began at a little stream that brawled noisily down from the steep peaks and ran through a new graveyard, where rude crosses tilted haphazardly this way and that, and headboards improvised from shingles were already sinking into the sod.

Hagar rode in past the graveyard, looking down a long, double line of flaring kerosene torches hung in front of the saloons and honky-tonks and deadfalls that had mushroomed here. The noise of the town was like surf beating roughly on a rocky shore. It was not a new sound for Hagar.

For a long time there had been rumors that the Union

Pacific was going to build a spur north through the Laramies to the Montana gold fields. That and the opening of new land and a high cattle market had made a boom for War Bonnet in the year of its short existence. Hagar counted six saloons in the first block. The hitching racks were crowded with mud-clotted cow ponies, and the boardwalks swayed and clattered to the constant ebb and flow of the crowd.

Hagar passed a new building, lifting its three stories above the clamor. Paint had run from the curlicues of a sign that announced it as the **Pioneer House**. At its door a pitchman had set up his thimble rig and was gathering a gaping crowd of high-heeled cowhands and red-shirted bullwhackers. Half a block farther down a frock-coated preacher stood on a shaky box, his hoarse voice pouring fire and brimstone on the knot of gaping men surrounding him. Hagar ran up against a line of immense Murphy wagons, piled high with their freight, and was forced right against the rumps of the ponies at the racks. They began cowkicking at his horse, and he had to fight his way down a full block of this before he was free again.

Then, from among the signs crowding business fronts along both sides of the street, he found another sign: **Sheriff's Office**. He pinched the buckskin in between the other horses at a rack and slid off, stretching his long legs gratefully. He looped reins over the rack and stepped onto the boardwalk, scraping viscid spring mud from his boots at the curb.

A pinch-faced man with a small deputy's badge sat in front of a desk with his boots up on it, spurs gouging the wood. He was cleaning a long-barreled Colt Peacemaker by the light of a single, flickering lamp on the desk at his elbow, and he nodded indifferently.

Hagar told him about Carter John, acutely aware of the peculiar odor that always seemed to characterize these surroundings—something compounded of yellowing **Wanted** posters, gun oil, and the dank reek of nearby cell blocks. The deputy worked a rag into the muzzle of his weapon.

"The sheriff's down at Cheyenne on county business. I'll tell him about it, when he gets back."

"But you'll bring the man in, give him a decent burial?"

"No hurry." The deputy peered with satisfaction down the barrel of his gun. "You said you piled rocks on him. He'll keep. We been burying so many around here the furniture store has run out of coffins. Just give me your name and where you'll be staying, in case we want to locate you."

"Paul Hagar's the name. I just got in. Maybe you can tell me a good place to stay."

"Pioneer House is the best place in town for the money."

"I'll be there, then."

Hagar left the place, grateful for fresh air. The deputy's callous indifference had left him with an edgy feeling. But he was remembering the graveyard, so big for a town only a year old, and knew he should not be surprised. A man could soon become inured to violence and death in a town like this. The ceaseless waves of noise closed around him again—the loud talk and the tinny music from a dozen saloons, the squeaking obbligato of their batwing doors swinging incessantly with the passage of men, the clattering tattoo of boots stamping along wooden walks. He knew he did not have much time left before the stage arrived, or the first wave of riders who had left Laramie as soon as the news of the opening broke. He asked a towering cowhand where the Land Office was, and the man pointed to a rickety frame building next to a feed barn a block down. As Hagar shouldered his way through the crowd, he saw a light against its window. He could see no line before that door, however, and his apprehension was eased. As he crossed the porch fronting the Land Office, he became aware of the man standing in the black maw of the feed barn. Perhaps it was the calico vest that made him stand out. He had his thumbs hooked in its armholes and was watching Hagar intently.

Still looking at the man, Hagar pulled open the door. Something tugged sharply at his pants leg. He glanced down to see that the quirt he had stuffed in his boot had caught on the door and had been pulled out. He had completely forgotten about it.

He picked it off the floor, realizing he should take it to the sheriff's office. It would do him no good to walk around with the quirt of a murdered man in his boot. Before he could turn, a door behind the waist-high counter opened and a man came through hurriedly, nervously shoving the cuffs of his clerk's alpaca jacket.

Hagar turned to him. "I just got in from Laramie. I'd like to see. . . ."

The expression on the man's face cut him off. Bilious yellow skin stretched tightly over bony cheeks as the clerk stared at the quirt.

"I thought Garland was sending his nephew," he said.

"Carter John?"

"Of course, Carter John. What happened?"

Wariness gave Hagar's face that hawkish look. "You might say he was held up."

The man was staring at the E Bar G engraved on the gold head of the quirt. "That's the identification, all right."

Habit, and a growing sense of the implications in this, made Hagar play it close to his vest. "It's Garland's quirt, isn't it?"

18

The clerk nodded sharply. "He said that would be it. I wish to hell you hadn't taken so long. I've had the papers ready since early this morning. The commissioner's due on the evening stage. We've got to get this done and get you out of here." He opened a drawer and brought out forms, arranging them hurriedly. "Grab that pen. It's got to be done in triplicate."

Hagar looked down at the top copy. Letters and numbers, meaningless in themselves, leaped out at him:

T. 4 S1, R. 6 W., Wyoming
Sec. 30, NE ¼ NE ¼, SE ¼ NE ¼,
NE ¼ SE ¼, SE ¼ SE ¼

It was already stamped with the date of May 30, 1886.

"How about pointing out the location on the map?" Hagar suggested.

The clerk made an exasperated sound, turning to snatch up a pointer and tap one of the big wall maps. "Right there. A hundred and sixty acres running in a saddle right across War Bonnet Pass."

Hagar pointed higher on the map. "That's north of the quarter section. What kind of land?"

"Mountains." Impatience gnawed at the clerk's voice. "Still government land, but the best summer graze in the Laramies. Now, damn it, will you sign . . . ?"

Hagar pointed lower on the map. "And south of the quarter section?"

"The flats. War Bonnet Valley. Winter graze for all the outfits around here."

"And in order to get their cattle up from the flats to summer graze, the ranchers have to go through the pass."

"That's right. And whoever owns the quarter section

controls the pass." The clerk shoved the pen angrily into his fingers. "Will you sign this, dammit? What the hell are you trying to do? A few more minutes and it'll be too late. If the commissioner finds you here, the whole thing will blow up."

Hagar was aware of a dryness in his throat, a throb of blood through his temples, as he saw the full import of what he was being handed. This was what Carter John had been coming north for, then. And Garland had given him that quirt to identify himself. And somebody had been willing to kill Carter John to stop him from signing. That made this strange offer valuable, and dangerous.

Hagar weighed the one against the other. He saw suspicion squinting the clerk's eyes and knew he had to make his decision at once. The man's feverish rush had kept him from the doubts he might have felt under ordinary circumstances, but they would not stay out of his mind much longer.

Hagar put the pen to paper. He had come north, looking for the main chance, hadn't he? And he was being handed the biggest chance of all. It had been a long time since he had speculated on such a level.

He signed his name, taking care to make it big and boldly legible.

Hagar stabled his horse at Whitworth's Livery after it was over. When he came from the stable, he saw that the windows of the Land Office were dark. So the whole thing had been set up just for this, and now he held a hot potato.

He struggled across the muddy bog of the street, gaining the boardwalk on the opposite side with ooze dripping off his boots, and headed toward the Pioneer House. He was turning the legal aspects of the thing over in his mind now.

The Laramie *Eagle* had announced that the land would be open for filing on May Thirty-First, tomorrow. Yet the date on the papers he had just signed was May Thirtieth. If tomorrow was the legal date of the opening, the clerk would not have been foolish enough to register the sale as of today. It would have been too damning a proof that an illegal transfer had been made.

Then the Thirtieth—today—was the true opening date for filing, and somehow the *Eagle* had made a mistake and set it ahead a day. That left Hagar's possession of the land valid, as far as the government was concerned. How the situation had been set up, how the true opening date had been kept secret, didn't bother him. His coattails were clean. He was simply the innocent bystander who had walked in to ask for information.

He swung through the door of the Pioneer House, saddlebags slung over one shoulder, and went to the desk. Rooms were two dollars a night, a little more than he had planned on, but he knew he couldn't get anything much cheaper in a boom town. It was a meagerly furnished room on the second floor with an iron bedstead, a single, rickety chair, a cracked, china bowl on a washstand. He washed and shaved, and afterward sat down to study carefully the triplicate copy of the government form the clerk had handed him when he had paid the filing fee. As far as Hagar could tell, it was in order. He beat as much dust and mud from his coat as possible, slipped into it, and went back downstairs.

At the desk, he asked for an envelope. He put the government papers in it, sealed it, addressed it to himself, and dropped it into the mail slot beneath the counter. A hot potato would be much safer with the United States Mail than on his person or in his room.

The dining room was down a pair of steps from the small lobby, a large chamber crammed with tables, filled with the clatter of utensils, the hoarse talk of a predominantly male dinner crowd. Hagar saw that there was but one empty table left, by the window, and went over to it. He slacked down into the chair, building a cigarette. The waitress came with the menu—a surprisingly prim and decent-looking woman for this rough town, her calico skirts making a homey rustle amid all the babble. He ordered the steak dinner, with coffee right away, and she left him. He noticed then that she had been blocking off a man who had just entered from the cramped lobby. He was a little man in a black frock coat, his marseilles waistcoat wrinkled across his comfortable girth. He had a pale face, his forehead was a gleaming dome, his china-blue eyes held the bland guilelessness of a child as he surveyed the room. They lit on the empty chair at Hagar's table, and asked their question. Hagar dipped his head in-differently, and the man came over.

"You are kind, sir. And a stranger, too."

Hagar's smile rose briefly to his face. "How can you tell . . . in a town like this?"

The man chuckled, scraping back the chair, carefully spreading the tails of his coat before seating himself. "A man keeps his eyes open. It pays me to know what goes on in War Bonnet. I'm Napoleón Nicholet, and up to now the only representative of the legal profession between here and Laramie. Nicholet through a dubious French descent. Napoleón from the whim of a slightly unbalanced uncle who laid questionable claim to a rank under the First Consul and who seemed to cherish the hope that I would make this land my Elba and return to restore France to her former glory. I must have disappointed him greatly. My only empire consists of a miserable law office in Douglas, an

22

Appaloosa named Josephine, and a parrot named Marshal Ney."

A question rose cherubically into the lawyer's eyes. He pursed his lips, waiting, and Hagar said: "Paul Hagar. Not representative of anything much, I guess."

The man chuckled again, tucking the napkin under his chin with pale, almost womanish hands. "You represent more than you realize, my friend. The surging tide of westward expansion. The new blood of America. All the glorious violence, the heroism, even the greed . . . ," he broke off, leaning forward. "Do you really think you'll make a killing off land like that?"

Surprise left its definite shock in Hagar. He could not help the flutter of his eyes. Then wariness closed down. He felt it contract the muscles of his face, leaving a wooden expression there.

"You assume a lot," he said.

Nicholet smiled blandly. "Perhaps you were a cattleman once, but that was long ago. Those rope burns on your hands are old. And you couldn't be any of the railroad men. They have a rate down at the Platte Hotel. Dust on your pants. A long ride. Why else would you make a long ride at this time? The land, and only the land." He slapped the table triumphantly.

Hagar relaxed, allowing himself to smile, realizing the man was only generalizing. "You should be a detective."

"A lawyer must be many things," Nicholet said, with a pleased chortle. "I'm right, then. You are a speculator."

"Aren't we all, in one way or another?"

Nicholet lost his humor, toying with his knife and fork. "Perhaps you'll be disappointed. The government's been claiming they'll open that section for years now. Some speculators mapped out this town three years ago on the basis of it and lost their shirts. Took the railroad to bring it into existence."

Hagar was not listening. A woman had come to the entryway and stopped there to survey the dining room. Lamplight threaded flecks of gold through her high-piled hair. An emerald-green dress made a Junoesque statue of her body. There was hardly a man in the room who hadn't turned to stare. But her eyes had stopped at Hagar. They were big eyes, made even bigger with her astonishment. Finally they became heavy-lidded again, and she picked up her long skirt in one hand and came through the tables toward him. *Like a queen,* he thought, and the years crowded in on him. He felt himself shove his chair back and stand up. She nodded this way and that at men who greeted her, without taking her wondering gaze off Hagar.

Then she was before him, with the tenebrous perfume of her turning the world to spring around him. "How long has it been, Paul?"

"Five years, Cheryl," he said. His voice sounded thick and strange. "Your dad with you?" How painful to be so prosaic. Yet what more would he have said, if they had been alone?

"Dad died two years ago, Paul."

His sense of inadequacy deepened. "I'm sorry." He tried to find more words, but couldn't.

She must have seen his helplessness. She smiled reassuringly, a little sadly. "I know, Paul. I wish you could have been at his funeral. Dad always liked you." She paused. "Dad had bought a lot here, in the original townsite. I used his insurance to build the hotel on it."

"It's quite a place."

"Is it, Paul?" A million strange things stirred in her eyes, studying him so quietly, and then she lifted her chin with a quick little breath, turning impulsively to the lawyer. "I'm sorry, Mister Nicholet."

The man bowed. "Quite all right, my dear. When two old . . . friends are reunited, the world stands still." He let his eyes move from Cheryl to Hagar, as if trying to gauge what lay between them. "Isn't it strange, how we can never escape our past?"

"Yes." She was still looking at Hagar. "Isn't it?" One of her eyebrows arched upward in that quizzical habit he knew so well. "In War Bonnet on business, Paul?"

"I thought there might be an opportunity here."

"Speculating in land, perhaps?"

"Perhaps."

He saw the wry humor leave her face, saw the disappointment settle its shadowed hollows beneath her cheeks. "Nothing's changed, then, with you."

"Did you think it would?"

Her voice held a wooden quality. "I suppose I hoped."

"What if I had changed? Would it have made any difference?"

A deeply indrawn breath swelled her mature breasts, and for a moment the expression of her eyes looked almost stricken. He supposed, however, that he was reading too much into it. He always seemed to, with her. Her weight settled, and she tilted her head toward Nicholet. "You'll have to excuse us again."

"Perhaps I'm in the way," the lawyer said.

Before she could answer, someone coming through the maze of the tables caught Cheryl's attention, and she half turned. Hagar saw that it was a man in a black clawhammer coat. He had the deceptive slimness of a steel blade and a blank, frozen face. Only the eyes held life. They were jet black, unwinking, the pupils contracted, like a cat's in

25

rage, to almost pin-point intensity. He nodded to Cheryl, murmuring greeting.

"Miss Bannister. I didn't mean to interrupt. I've been looking for Nicholet."

Hagar saw Cheryl's lips tuck in at the corners with that sign of distaste he knew so well. "That's all right, Poker," she said stiffly. "I'd like you to meet Paul Hagar. Paul . . . Russian Poker."

He felt her dislike coloring his own voice, for their attitudes, their reactions had run so parallel, except for that one great thing. "Russian Poker," he said. "Sounds like a game."

The man faced him. "It is. Perhaps you'd like to go a round."

Cheryl spoke sharply. "Poker . . . !"

"A new face, a new reaction," Poker said. His voice had taken on a metallic quality. "Perhaps here's one with more spirit. I begin to lose faith. I begin to think there aren't any of the true hearts left in the world. What has happened to all the gamblers? It's supposed to be an instinct in man as deep as hunger. Where is it, now? In the clods of this town? Even Nicholet has failed me."

"Mister Hagar came north on speculation," Nicholet said slyly.

"Please . . . ," Cheryl began.

"How fascinating," Poker said, breaking in on Cheryl again. He leaned toward Hagar, the pupils of his eyes distended. "How much of a speculator are you, Mister Hagar?"

Nicholet's lips were pursed in ironic relish as he looked at Hagar's hawk-like face. "From the looks of him, he has been speculating most of his life, and in almost everything."

"Nicholet, Poker . . . !" Cheryl's voice held growing exasperation. "You're going too far. Not in my dining room."

"Please, Cheryl." Although Poker addressed her, he was

still watching Hagar. Like a hungry cat watching a mouse. "Just one round. It's been so long since anybody worth his salt would go with me." He snaked a five-shot house gun from beneath a lapel with a surprising flash of movement and flipped out the cylinder with a practiced flirt of his wrist, spilling the five cartridges into his palm. Then he thumbed one bullet back in, closed the cylinder, and spun it.

"Here, Hagar. You first."

Cheryl's lips were pinched and white. "Poker, if you don't put that away this instant . . . !"

"You hesitate," Poker told Hagar. He seemed deaf to Cheryl, oblivious of her existence. Sweat shone on his forehead, and a strange excitement glazed his eyes. "I'll go the first round, then," he said. "I was only trying to be polite."

He lifted the gun till its muzzle touched his temple. Cheryl started to speak again, but only a breath left her parted lips, a hopeless, sighing, little sound. Hagar realized he was holding his breath, realized that all the noises of the room had stopped, that every eye was turned toward Poker. The man's eyes were wide and shining, the pupils immensely distended. A little muscle twitched in his cheek.

He pulled the trigger.

The sharp, metallic *click* seemed to be inside Hagar, giving him an emotional jolt so strong he felt as if his whole body jerked. Smiling—a taut, jeering grimace—Poker lowered the gun again. He lifted a hand to wipe the sweat from his brow. Slowly his pupils contracted, the strange ecstasy fading from his eyes.

"There," he said in a breathless voice. "What greater gamble could you take, Hagar? It's the only logical thing left . . . to a man who has gambled on everything else. Try it."

He held out the gun. Then he frowned, letting it slowly drop back to his side. Hagar could hear it, too, now. The noise in the street. It rose out of the ordinary street sounds like a mounting, hysterical roar. Someone yelled in the lobby.

A man at a far table turned, shouting: "What?" Then he jumped up, kicking over his chair. Others followed him. The dining room was filled with the clatter of overturned chairs, the shriek of sliding tables, the yelling of men. It became a rout. The whole crowd jammed in the door, pouring outside. But one was coming back in, fighting his way through the press with his elbows. A squat man with a flat, scarred face, his muscles bulging beneath a turtle-necked jersey. When he saw Poker, he began shouting.

"Poker, something went wrong! The land commissioner just rode in from Douglas with the sheriff. He's raising hell. The date for the opening of that government grass was the Thirtieth. This morning. The Land Office is going to be opened up again right away."

"What the hell are you coming in here for?" Poker shouted. "Get out and stop that line. Break it up somehow. We've got to get Calico in there first."

"He's there," the other man said hoarsely. "I've had him hanging around that office for a week."

Poker began to kick his way through the overturned chairs. "Damn you, if he doesn't make it, I'll. . . ." He broke off suddenly, glancing back at Cheryl and Hagar. Something furtive ran through his eyes, and he went on out swiftly. The room was left empty, except for the three of them at the window.

Nicholet chuckled softly. "You'd think he let a big cat out of the bag."

"How could he think we wouldn't know what they planned?" Cheryl said disgustedly. "The whole town's known for months."

Nicholet sighed. "It's been rightly named the Bloody

Quarter. It has the only approach to Big Squaw Creek. On either flank are bluffs, rising a hundred feet over Big Squaw. There is no cut between those bluffs on the opposite bank. The creek rises from underground somewhere up in the Laramie Mountains. Between its source and that point, the watercourse consists almost entirely of falls and rapids and deep chasms which render it inaccessible for watering any stock. Directly south are the Alkali Buttes. The water running through there is so full of alkali it would eat holes in your stomach as big as my *chapeau*. I saw a mule drink there once. When they found it dead later, it took them an hour to decide what kind of animal it had been." He broke off, turning to Hagar. "Hadn't you better get in line?"

Hagar looked out the window at the scene in the street, turned bizarre by the light of a hundred kerosene torches. Over the heads of the running mob he could see the queue already forming at the Land Office, twisted back and forth like a wagging tail by the constant surge of the crowds all around it. Next door to the Pioneer House the boardwalk had collapsed, pitching a dozen men into the mud. Another knot of running men had overturned a spring buggy in its wild rush across the street, and none of the men was making any attempt to help the woman who had been spilled out. Hagar had seen gold put the same craze in men. For a moment he had the impulse to play his part, to join the rush, unwilling to reveal himself so soon. Then he realized that the whole town would know who had got the Bloody Quarter as soon as Russian Poker's man tried to file. He let a bleak smile cross his face, saying: "A little late now, isn't it?"

Nicholet glanced out of the window at the crowd, and then looked back to Hagar. "Perhaps it is," he said, in the softest of voices. Suspicion was clouding his eyes. "Perhaps it's later than we think."

29

Chapter Three

When Hagar went up to his room at ten, the shuffling line extended out of sight down the main street, and he knew it would still be there when he came back for breakfast. He would never cease to marvel at what hunger for land could do to men. The street was choked with rigs and saddle mounts, and there was a constant stir of movement as men and women hurried from the Land Office to disentangle their animals and head outward into the night toward the acreage they had filed on.

Hagar had lingered over dinner. Beginning to realize the full value of what he held, he had half expected Poker to return with a bid. But the man had not shown up. Nicholet had eaten with him, filling the meal with sly innuendoes, which Hagar had parried disinterestedly, and had then gone, leaving Hagar alone in the dining room. After dinner he had a drink, a smoke, another drink. Still no approach. Finally, beaten down by the long day, he decided to go upstairs. It was dark enough in the hall to see the thin line of light under his door. He halted, thinking a moment. If it were a trap, they wouldn't leave the light to warn him. He tried the knob and swung the door open wide without stepping in, one hand on his gun.

Cheryl Bannister was sitting close to the lamp on the ivory-topped table, and its heat filled her face with a faint flush. The deep, startling blue of her eyes had always held a disturbing, searching quality, when there was no humor on her face. She gazed up at him, unsmiling, her hands on her lap. He stepped inside, closing the door behind him.

"Always the direct approach," he said.

"It's my hotel. I didn't think you'd mind."

"I'm flattered." He stood in the middle of the room, studying her, and felt the nostalgia touch him again. "You were a little girl," he said. "A little, snub-nosed girl with freckles and skinny legs and pigtails. You had to stand on a box to wash dishes in your mother's boarding house. And still you only came up to my chin, when I dried for you."

"Is that what you remember?"

"It's nice to remember."

"No other pictures?"

"I guess I don't want to remember them."

She drew a deep breath. "I can't say I blame you. It was rather stormy the last time, wasn't it?"

"You seem quieter now."

"We all change a little, Paul."

"Do we? You told me I could never change, Cheryl. A fiddlefoot. A drifter."

The color grew deeper in her soft cheeks. "Was I wrong?"

He knew a quick anger and walked to the window, shoving it open hard. The wind ruffled his coat and caught at the edges of his jet black hair, carrying with it the odors of rank mud and pine and new spring grass. He stared down at the crowded street.

"You wouldn't be angry unless I'd struck the truth, Paul," she said. "You'd be surprised to learn how much I know of you . . . these last years. Freighting in Santa Fé. That two-bit gold rush down near Camarillo. Even a hitch in the Army."

"How many spies do you have?" he said, without turning.

Her laugh was a little rueful, plucking at his nerves with its throaty promise. "Missouri Carnes has been through here a couple of times lately. He's some kind of advance man for the railroad. He told me he'd seen you in Tucson. He didn't think you looked good in uniform."

"That's Missouri," Hagar said. "I haven't seen him since then. It's funny to remember how close the three of us were."

"And now," she said, "you have the Bloody Quarter."

He turned around, wariness giving his face the hawk-like edge. "They know, then," he said.

She nodded. "Russian Poker had a man named Calico waiting to file on the Bloody Quarter. They had to knock in a couple of heads to get Calico first in line. It didn't do them much good, did it?"

"What's Poker's interest in that quarter section?"

She frowned at him. "You're asking me?"

"I am."

She studied him a moment, puzzled. "Russian Poker heads the gambling interests in War Bonnet, Paul," she said. "They call themselves the Syndicate, and they're about the most powerful single force in town. In fact, politically, they run the town. Now they're after the county."

"I thought Ed Garland was the strong man in county politics."

"He was . . . till last year. This was all Albany County, then. The county seat was Laramie. That's the center of Garland's power. But the county was too big, too unwieldy, and, when the move began to cut it in two, Garland didn't have enough power up here to stop it."

Hagar knew about that. The upper half of Albany County had become Converse County, with War Bonnet as its seat. "I guess Garland has been fighting ever since to get back in power up here," he said.

She nodded. "And the Syndicate has done everything in its power to stop him. Up to now it's been a stalemate. You can see how important the Bloody Quarter becomes. Outside of the gamblers, the only other group with any power is the ranchers. Whoever has their support is a long way toward control of the county."

"And a man owning the Bloody Quarter controls that pass to all their high graze."

Again she nodded. "That's right. It's been fought over before. Garland tried to keep the ranchers from going through last year. Several men were killed. But he had no legal claim, and, when the smell reached the legislature, he had to stop."

"But a man with legal claim could keep the ranchers from going through," Hagar murmured.

"Yes. You can see what a powerful hold he'd have over them. They'd almost have to do as he said. It means their very existence." She frowned again. "They certainly didn't tell you much of the situation."

"Who didn't?"

"It's not like you to walk in on something so blind."

His eyes grew heavy-lidded. "How did the gambling Syndicate ever come to pick a fool like that for its head?"

Her face tightened. "Don't underestimate Poker. He might have some sort of obsession about that game. I guess he goes a little crazy, when he plays it. But it's his only weakness. On anything else, he's deadly."

"Is it really a weakness?" he said.

Her eyes dropped momentarily, in a studying way. "Other people have thought he might be faking. I don't think so, Paul. Nobody's that good an actor. Couldn't it really get into your blood that way?"

"If you were a little crazy to begin with, maybe," he said. "How about Nicholet?"

"One of the decent men in War Bonnet. He's handled the legal business for the ranchers so long that he's become sort of a spokesman for them, almost their nominal head. They meant to try to file on the Bloody Quarter, too. Probably had a man waiting. They'll be bitterly disappointed." She raised her eyes again. "When Nicholet found out for sure that you'd filed on the Bloody Quarter, he thought you were fronting for somebody, too."

"What did you tell him?"

"I told him the Paul Hagar I knew would never front for anybody. You were probably in this for a quick killing, and then you'd move on. You never stayed anywhere long."

He felt anger stain his cheeks again. Here it was once more, coming between them, as it had so often before. Why did it have to mean so much? Was she really right? Could he never change? "Maybe you were wrong, Cheryl. Maybe I won't move on."

She rose so swiftly it startled him, a wild hope shining in her eyes. Then she checked herself, withdrawing into something more than past disappointment. "You've told me that before."

He brought himself in close, catching her elbows, till the silken curve of her deep breast was a pressure against him. "What if I meant it this time?" he asked thickly.

She shook her head, a subdued torture in her eyes, turning her face away from him at last. "It wouldn't matter, Paul. It wouldn't matter."

He realized now what he had only sensed in her before, something putting a greater gap between them than that one fundamental gulf. He let his hands slide slowly off her arms. "There's another man."

She would not look at him. Her eyes were squinted, the lashes wet with tears. She nodded her head once. He stepped back, and he couldn't keep the thread of cynicism from his voice. "A good, solid citizen. Pillar of the community. Feet planted on the ground. Never move on. . . ."

"Don't, Paul." Her voice broke.

He took a long breath. "I'm sorry, Cheryl."

She turned and walked to the door. She opened it, and then paused. Tears still shone in her eyes. Her profile was a softly molded thing with the fruit-like curve of her cheek, the tremulous satin of her underlip. He did not think her ripened beauty had ever struck him so poignantly.

"I'm sorry you came, Paul," she said, without looking at him. "Whether you're holding it for yourself or for somebody else, the Bloody Quarter is a terribly dangerous possession. Get rid of it as quickly as possible. Please."

A bleak look turned his face gaunt. "I guess I'm sorry I came, too, Cheryl," he said emptily. "But not because of the Bloody Quarter."

Chapter Four

Hagar pounded down the last of his notice stakes and heaped up small rocks at the base so it would be sure to stay in place. This was in accordance with law, the first necessary step in securing title to the land. It had taken up the whole of this first afternoon spent on the quarter section.

He stepped back, wiping sweat from his forehead. The mountains rolled away on every side, steep and rugged, cloaked with timber so dense it looked black in many places. To any man who knew cattle, it was obvious that they could not be moved across those peaks in any numbers with anything short of a derrick and tackle. The only route through was the pass, below him. His land ran from this ridge down into that pass and straight across to the first ridge on the other side. From this eminence Hagar could see the trail at the bottom of the pass, crossing the line his stakes marked, running on down toward the flats, with a dozen feeder trails funneling into it. The whole story of his situation lay in that picture. It was hard for him to realize fully, even now, that he held the fate of almost every cattleman in War Bonnet in his hands.

He mounted his horse and turned her back toward the shack, dropping down through clumps of quaking aspen and stunted spruce, across meadows of springy buffalo grass whose green mantles were splashed with the riotous color of buttercups and cowslip and verbena. It struck him that, aside from its political value, this was a good piece of land.

Such transient sense of proprietorship drew a cynical smile from him as he remembered the scene between Cheryl and himself last night. It hadn't been as stormy as that scene in Denver, five years ago, the last time he had asked her to marry him. But it had been the same, with the same gulf lying between them. Five years ago he had made an exceptionally good strike on cattle speculation, but that hadn't meant much to her. What he planned to do with the strike was more important. So he had bought the livery stable and had made a fiasco of the whole business. Why was it that a man couldn't even settle down when he wanted to?

Or maybe he hadn't wanted to—badly enough. There had been books to keep, and he hadn't done much about that. There had been too many friends drifting into town without the price of a stall, or feed, or of even a room for themselves. It seemed half his stalls had been filled with that kind. Then there had been that rumor of a new gold strike up at Aspen Creek. . . .

He shook his head. What a young fool he'd been! The worst part was asking Cheryl to marry him, even after he'd failed. And now he was five years older, and still a fool. The habits of all his life still clung, the things that had molded him could not let him out of that mold. And it wouldn't matter if they could. *There's another man.*

He felt sodden in the saddle with the sense of defeat that the thought brought him. His lips thinned as he tried to drive it from his mind, as he drew up to the shack he had found that morning. It was in a pocket, beyond a spring that bubbled from under a rock ledge. Not much of a cabin— probably started as a soddy by some trappers longer ago than anybody could remember, kept up a little by trail drivers bringing their beef north from Texas. Hagar had lashed a couple of fresh poles onto the corral out back. He turned his horse in here, stripping it, carrying the gear into the shack. Some of the chinking was gone from the pole walls, but that could be patched with mud and moss. The sheet-iron stove was black with rust, but its chimney still drew. There was a shuck pad on the chicken wire stretched for a bunk. A man could make out in it.

Hagar's gun was heavy against his leg, and he unbelted it and hung it on a peg where it would be within reach while he made supper. He put coffee on the stove and shaved bacon into a skillet. There was a rickety table, and he moved his holstered gun to it before he sat down. He ate leisurely, watching through the open door as dusk turned distant ridges to billows of smoke, and then blotted them out entirely. The air grew chilly, and he closed the door, when he was through with the meal. The fire was dying, and he moved over to the fresh wood he had chopped and stacked next to the bunk.

Somebody kicked open the door.

Hagar wheeled. But he was caught. The man took two lunging steps into the room and stopped—between Hagar and his holstered gun on the table.

They stood there, facing each other, and even the sound of their breathing had died on the air. Then the man let his breath out in a sardonic little chuckle, and the upheld tension of his great body settled down. But he did not take his hand off the worn, bone handle of the six-shooter stuck naked through his belt.

He was big in every direction, inches taller than Hagar, inches broader, with a flat-topped hat set back at an arrogant angle on curly hair so black it looked blue. There was a rough belligerence in his flat, hard muscles, his smoky eyes, the flaring nostrils of his pugnacious Irish nose.

"Patrick Drumgriffin," he said. "Out of Ireland, out of county Meath, where the colleens are sweeter and the peat's blacker and the quickthorns grow higher than anywhere else in the world."

Hagar realized his body was still held in a little crouch, and he straightened up. A corner of his vision momentarily caught on his Henry repeater, in its boot, where he had dumped the saddle and blankets at the door. But it was three feet behind Drumgriffin.

"Do I have to introduce myself?" he said ironically.

"No, Hagar," Drumgriffin said. "You don't." He tilted his head to one side, calling: "Willows?"

Another man stepped into the door and moved to one side, a weedy cowpuncher in dirty range clothes, chewing sourly on plug tobacco that bulged one weather-roughened cheek.

Drumgriffin said: "This is Mister Paul Hagar, Jack. He came into War Bonnet a day early, speculating on land, and he should have known better than to take what he found."

Jack Willows spat into the fire. "Yeah," he said.

"You can come in, Ed," Drumgriffin said, raising his voice. "We've pulled his teeth."

There was a moment of silence. A horse snorted outside. Then the third man entered.

He was only a little above medium height. Powerful shoulders and a leonine head made him seem taller. His Stetson must have cost fifty dollars, his suit six times that much. Yet the broadcloth coat and trousers were dirty and rumpled, the bench-made boots were worn and muddy. This paradox was partially explained by his face. A life in the open had burned it the color of old oak. His blue eyes were paled by the sun and were held in a habitual squint. Here was a man who had come up the hard way, and no amount of riches would soften him, would make him lose the rough heritage of his beginnings. He probably still spent every roundup with his crews, still felt uncomfortable within four walls. Here, Hagar knew without asking, was Ed Garland.

He studied Hagar narrowly for a minute. "You look tough," he said.

"Not so tough," grinned Drumgriffin.

"Do you have the papers with you?" Garland asked.

"How much are you offering?"

"Offering, hell!" Garland said. "I didn't come here to make any deal with a damn' drifter who got in this whole thing by mistake. You'll sign those papers over to me and leave here tonight. You'll get clear out of Wyoming and count yourself damn' lucky to be alive."

Hagar smiled faintly. "I've heard you worked like that. Did you use the same tactics with the *Eagle*? It printed May Thirty-First as the opening date for filing on this land. The commissioner said it was the Thirtieth. How could the *Eagle* have made such a mistake?"

"A printer's error," Garland said thinly.

"Or an editor's?" Hagar asked. "The editor of the *Eagle* is an old friend of mine, Garland. Not bad, as men go. Somewhat of a realist, though. If the biggest stockholder in his paper told him to make a mistake on a date, and maybe added some financial attraction, he'd do it without too much fuss. Do you own stock in the *Eagle*, Garland?"

A touch of grudging humor made a flinty gleam in Garland's sun-faded eyes. "What if I do?"

"So you got a day's advantage because of the *Eagle*'s error and you sent somebody to file on this quarter during that day. You couldn't file yourself. Nobody owning as much land as you is eligible for a homestead. What happened to the man you sent?"

The transitory humor was gone from Garland's eyes, and his voice lowered to a silken hiss. "I thought maybe you'd know."

Hagar studied the man's face narrowly. It was a safe bet that Garland did not yet know his nephew was dead. He would have shown more rage, more hatred than this. And if he had just come north from Laramie, it was more than likely he had only stopped in War Bonnet long enough to find out what had happened to the Bloody Quarter.

"All I know is the land clerk mistook me for the man you were sending," Hagar said.

Garland's brows pulled in tightly. "I can't quite believe that."

Hagar realized the man was thinking of the identification. He knew it would be pointless to bring it up now, and probably dangerous.

"The man you sent was a day late," Hagar said. "The land commissioner was due any minute. That clerk was so jumpy he would have signed it over to a jackass, if it had said the right thing."

"And you said the right thing?" Garland's voice was sarcastic.

"I said I was from Laramie. Apparently nobody else had been in from there all day. It was a logical assumption on the clerk's part. I've played enough poker. When I saw what he was driving at, I went along with it." Hagar stared intently at Garland. "What's your stake in this? You own half of Wyoming already."

"Something bigger than you could ever understand. They thought they could pull a smart play up here, cutting the old Albany County in half. They thought they could get its votes and tip the balance against me in the state legislature." He turned to pace across the room, face tight with the pressure of something built up to the bursting point. "They won't get away with it. Poker's Syndicate can't do anything without the ranchers behind them. And they won't have the ranchers. Not with me holding the Bloody Quarter."

"Whoever holds the Quarter holds Converse County," Hagar said.

"And whoever holds Converse County holds the state," Garland said. "That's the way it's set up."

"If it means so much, you should be willing to bid a good figure for this land."

Garland stopped pacing, his mouth twisting sickly. "Not one thin dime. This has cost me too much already. I want those papers, Hagar. You'll sign them over to me."

"Do you think I'd be fool enough to carry them around with me?"

Garland's eyes became slits. "You knew their value. You wouldn't trust them with anybody else."

"You won't find them here."

Garland took a long breath. "Pat," he said.

Drumgriffin smiled broadly and took a step toward Hagar. "You'd better hand them over, drifter."

"You'd better think twice, Drumgriffin."

"We're just gonna frisk you," the Irishman grinned. "And if we don't find 'em that way, we'll beat 'em out of you."

One instant he was still coming forward in that easy, smiling way, the next instant he was exploding right into Hagar. Hagar had never seen such blinding speed. A blow smashed him in the face. He felt himself pitch backward across the table, felt the table skid into the wall. He saw Drumgriffin closing in. Lying across the table, he grabbed its edge with both hands and doubled up both legs. Drumgriffin couldn't stop quick enough. He came into Hagar's spiked heels with his chest. Then Hagar straightened his legs with all the driving force in their lean length.

Drumgriffin pitched backward. Hagar followed him. Drumgriffin tried to stop himself at the door, but his hand only cracked the frame, and he went on through and crashed onto his back.

Both Willows and Garland had gone for their guns. But Hagar reached Willows before his was out, catching him by the shirt and swinging him around into Garland. The shirt ripped, but the man went into Garland anyway, knocking him back against the wall so hard the whole shack trembled.

Then Hagar went on out after Drumgriffin. But the Irishman hadn't got up. Still on his back, he had pulled his six-gun. It was pointed right at Hagar's belly, and it was cocked.

"Hold it, Pat."

The voice came from the timber to Drumgriffin's right. His face tightened. His body seemed to lift up. Then it settled back, finger trembling against the trigger in reaction. Hagar had stopped at the voice. He saw a shadowy form moving across the trees on a big white mare. It was Napoleón Nicholet, with a gun held steadily in one fist.

Hagar heard the shuffling movement in the shack behind him and stepped aside so he would not be silhouetted in the door. Drumgriffin got up, the ruddy anger seeping out of his truculent face. Garland came slowly out of the door, staring at Nicholet. Savage anger twisted at his mouth. He controlled it with palpable effort.

"I'll give you a chance to stay out of this, Nicholet," he said. "Put that gun away and ride out of here, and we'll forget what happened."

"You're the ones who are riding out," Nicholet said blandly.

"You fool!" Garland said thickly. "You don't know what you're doing."

"On the contrary." The lawyer smiled. "I am probably aware of more ramifications than you are. Now put the gun away, Pat, and get to your horse."

Drumgriffin stuck his gun back into his belt. He was not even looking at Nicholet. His eyes, still smoky with rage, were fixed on Hagar. "I'll see you again," he said.

Hagar's face remained blank. He held the Irishman's eyes without answering. Garland was still staring at Nicholet, his face white with suppressed anger. His lips parted. He started to speak.

"It won't do any good, Garland," the lawyer said. "The best thing you can do is get on your horse and leave here. You've made your bid, and it's fallen through."

"You won't stop me up here, Nicholet," Garland said. His voice had a strangled sound. "And when I get Converse County, you're the first man I'm going to break."

Nicholet's bald brows raised archly, but he did not answer. With a frustrated sound, Garland turned toward his horse, followed by Willows and Drumgriffin. There was the distant creak of leather, the snort of a horse. Nicholet chuckled, getting off his big animal.

"I'm obliged to you," Hagar said. "That Irishman was set to shoot."

"Only protecting my interests," Nicholet said. "As you know, I'm connected with the ranchers around here. We knew Poker had Calico waiting to be the first in line at the Land Office. We had a man of our own planted. Hoped to divert Calico with a fight in that feed barn and shove our own man in ahead. But none of us knew the definite date when the land would be open for filing. That's where you had the advantage on us. I half suspected you were fronting for Garland . . . till this evening." Nicholet became aware that he still held his gun, and slipped it back into the shoulder sling under his coat with a rueful expression. "I always feel awkward with this damn' thing. I wonder what would happen, if I really had to use it."

"How did you happen to be here tonight?" Hagar asked.

"The ranchers sent me with their offer for the Bloody Quarter," Nicholet explained. "Twenty-five hundred dollars cash, payable immediately."

Hagar frowned deeply. The offer was far too low. He studied the man's guileless face, unable to believe Nicholet didn't know it was too low. "Are you joking?" he asked.

Nicholet carefully removed his hat and rubbed a handkerchief around the inside of its sweatband. "Cash in hand, Hagar. Twenty-five hundred dollars more than Garland offered."

"How do you know what he offered?"

"I know the man. He never buys what he can take. This whole deal has already cost him a lot more than he'd care to admit. And you know cattlemen. They may be rich on paper, but half the year they haven't got a cent in the bank. Garland may be the richest man in this state, Hagar, but I've seen the time before a spring or a fall roundup when he couldn't get his hands on a hundred dollars cash money. That's the trouble with climbing. You're always one jump ahead of yourself."

"I think he can raise more than twenty-five hundred, if he sees there isn't any other way," Hagar said.

Nicholet shook his head. "You'll never get it from him. You'd better take my offer. It's all the ranchers can raise, and it's better than a bullet in the back."

"They'll have to scratch harder," Hagar said. "Don't they realize the consequences to them if Garland gains control of this pass?"

"Only too well." Nicholet sighed. "What figure did you have in mind?"

"Ten thousand dollars."

"You'll never get it."

"Russian Poker has yet to make his bid."

Nicholet shook his head. "Have you no scruples?"

"From what I've heard, I'd rather sell to the ranchers," Hagar said. "But I'm not going to sacrifice seventy-five hundred dollars just because they're nice people."

"I sympathize with you," Nicholet said.

"If they want to reconsider, I'll still be open to reason. But I can't wait too long. It's a hot potato, Nicholet."

"Are you in a hurry merely to sell . . . or to leave?"

Hagar's face darkened. "There's nothing to hold me here."

Nicholet's eyes flickered slyly. "I should think a woman like Cheryl Bannister would hold any man anywhere."

"That's over," Hagar said darkly.

"It didn't look that way from what I saw between you in the hotel dining room."

"Let it go, will you? There's another man."

"Did she tell you who?"

"No."

An ironic smile filled Nicholet's face. "Then I will. It's Patrick Drumgriffin."

Chapter Five

It rained during the night, and kept on well into the next day. Hagar stayed inside till it let up in the afternoon, and then rode into War Bonnet, with the dark clouds still tiered sullenly above the mountains. Center Street was a lane of shining mud, but the rain had not dimmed its sense of feverish activity. Carpenters' hammers banged furiously around the frame of a big building springing up on a corner lot. The high, fretful whine of a whipsaw came from beyond it. The hitching racks were crowded with rigs and horses and cow ponies bearing a dozen different brands. The boardwalks trembled and clattered to the incessant tramp of booted feet. Yet, there was something else. A man crossed the street ahead of him, the viscid, spring mud sucking at his boots with a hollow pop every time he took a step, and then he climbed onto the boardwalk and turned around to scrape the goo from his boots on the edge of the high curb. When he stopped that, he stood there, as if he had seen Hagar for the first time. Something crossed his face. Hagar was past before he could define the expression.

Hagar found a slot at a hitching rack and dismounted, making his tie, stepping up onto the high curb. Two doors down was a saloon with an ornate façade called Little Al's Place. A cowpuncher came out, wiping his hand across his mouth. The batwings hit him in the back as he stopped abruptly, staring at Hagar. Then he went across the walk and ducked beneath a rack and swung into a double-barreled stock saddle on a hairy black. As he wheeled the horse out, carelessly spraying mud, Hagar saw the E Bar G on its rump.

He stood a long moment, watching the rider disappear in the crowd down the street. Before he moved again, Cheryl Bannister came from the door of the War Bonnet Mercantile, on his left. She wore a blue cape, hooded over her gold-flecked hair, and carried a wicker basket over one arm. When she saw Hagar, a smile started to form on her ripe lips, and then faded. She came slowly to him and stopped.

"Nicholet told me you'd be in town today."

"There's a man who interests himself uncommonly in my comings and goings."

A touch of color stained her cheeks. "I'm sure he meant it only as a kindly gesture. He knew I was upset when I found you'd checked out of the hotel yesterday without . . . well, without even saying good bye."

"I thought maybe we'd said our good byes, Cheryl."

A breath deepened her breasts. She did not answer him for a moment. There was a faint scent about her, like a bank of violets after a shower. Crisp, golden ringlets peeped around her hood and made him remember how wet weather had always put curl into her hair. Suddenly her eyes dropped.

"I've been shopping for supper." Her voice sounded strained, hurried. "So many people keep pouring into town, I can't seem to buy enough of anything."

"I'll carry your basket."

Her eyes lifted again, holding a stricken look. "No, Paul. Please. . . ."

She broke off, seeing what was in his face. He studied her and finally nodded.

"I understand, Cheryl. Drumgriffin is in town."

Her lips parted. Her words were no more than a whisper. "You know?"

"Nicholet told me."

She frowned. "He told me you and Pat fought last night, but I didn't know it was over . . . over. . . ."

"Over you? It wasn't, Cheryl. I didn't even know he was the one, then." He took a deep breath, pinched lines forming about his eyes. "What kind of man is he, Cheryl? He doesn't look the type to have what I lacked. He looks wild, flamboyant, even more footloose than I was."

"He may be flamboyant. That's the Irish in him. But not footloose."

"Not as long as he's tied to Ed Garland's apron strings, anyway."

Cheryl flushed. "Pat is going to leave Garland soon. He's got a spread north of here. He's been stocking it up."

"From what I've seen of Garland, he won't like that."

"He knows Pat's plans. Pat's been a valuable man to him. Naturally he doesn't like the idea of losing him. But he can't stop Pat."

"It's funny," Hagar mused. "I wouldn't have suspected that combination in him. He looked like nothing more than a bully boy to me."

"You have to look underneath, Paul. He's got foundations . . . he's a hard worker."

"You don't have to defend him, Cheryl. If that's what you want, I wish you luck."

Her eyes shone suddenly, and she reached out to grasp his arm. "Thank you, Paul," she said huskily. "And please . . . don't have any more trouble with Pat."

"Think I'll get hurt?" he asked softly.

"You may have knocked him down last night," she said, "but that isn't the whole fight, Paul. I've seen you whip men I thought could kill you. But I've seen Pat fight, too. There isn't a man in War Bonnet who would face him barehanded." She broke off, shaking her head. "It wouldn't matter which of you won. You'd both be so broken up before you finished. . . ."

He caught her hand, smiling reassuringly. "All right, Cheryl. I'll stay out of his way . . . for your sake."

"Thank you again, Paul." She grew intensely sober, drawing her hand away. "Are you still speculating?"

"That's why I'm in town today. Where can I find Russian Poker?"

"You aren't going to sell to the ranchers, then?"

"I'll sell to the highest bidder."

"That doesn't sound like the man who couldn't make out in the livery business because his stalls were always filled with horses of friends who couldn't pay."

He hitched at his gun belt, his face hardening. "Don't try to make me out a saint, Cheryl. You know what I am. If the ranchers meet my price, I'll be glad to sell."

"They're the little men, Paul. Garland's the big man."

"And I'm standing right between, and, if I don't get rid of this hot potato soon, I'll get pinched off."

Disappointment shadowed her face, and the warmth was gone from her voice. "You'll find Russian Poker at Little Al's. Be careful, Paul. I know you've played dangerous games before. I don't think they ever matched this one."

Little Al's was in a new frame building, filled with the reek of muddy sawdust, raw whiskey, and stale cigar smoke. The pyramids of glassware on the back bar blinded Hagar with their glittering prisms as he swung through the door. At this hour most of the customers were drinking, and the roulette table and faro layouts at the rear were deserted except for a couple of shills, listlessly bucking the tiger to keep the game alive for some chance bystander who might wander in.

Over behind the round deal tables for poker, a ten-plate

stove glowed cherry red. Before it stood a man in a suit of rusty black, hands outstretched to the heat. His back was to the room, but his head was turned slightly so the slim cheroot was visible, tilted upward jauntily in his lips. Hagar knew only one man who smoked that way.

He found an empty stretch at the bar and hooked one heel in the brass rail, obliquely watching the man by the stove in the back-bar mirror. But the man did not turn around.

There were two bartenders, busily mixing drinks, and a third man, big and hearty, with a pomaded handlebar mustache, hair parted in the middle and plastered flat against his bulbous head, and blue eyes twinkling brightly from the pink rolls of beef forming his face. He came up to face Hagar, putting his blunt fingers on the bar like a pianist about to play.

"Welcome to Little Al's, stranger. You're in the best bar west of Omaha, and there's nothing you can't have. What's your pleasure? A pousse-café, maybe? A pisco punch? Stump me, and a bottle of my best whiskey is yours, with my compliments."

"Don't strain your brain, Al," Russian Poker said at Hagar's elbow. "Just make it three Little Al Specials, and bring them to number four."

Hagar turned, surprised.

A brief, humorless smile flitted across Poker's narrow face. "Don't say it. I walk like a cat. Back this way. We can talk business."

As Hagar passed down the bar behind the customers, none of them turned. But he could see their eyes, in the bar mirror, following him all the way to the rear. There was a row of numbered doors here. Poker opened number four and stepped in. Before he followed, Hagar glanced again toward the man at the stove. His back was still turned, his cheroot still tilted up.

"Friend of yours?" Poker asked.

"Not that I know of," Hagar said.

It was a small room with a lamp bracketed on each of the four walls, a table, and half a dozen rickety chairs. There was a pack of cards on the green topping of the table, an ash tray filled with old butts. Poker shoved them aside as he sat down. Hagar took a chair facing the door, his back to a blank wall.

The action drew another sardonic smile to Poker's lips. "Are you always that way?"

"Only on certain occasions."

Poker placed the tips of his fingers together, pursing his lips. "So you whipped Drumgriffin last night."

"It was just a brush."

Little Al came in with three drinks and set them on the table. He sat down. "You must have pulled some trick on him," he told Hagar. "I ain't seen the man yet that could whip that Irishman square."

Poker reached out and shoved back the cuff of Hagar's coat with the tip of his finger. He took the wrist between thumb and forefinger, turning it over. It was like the touch of a woman's hand.

"You're deceptive," he said. "From some angles you look narrow. But you've got big bones. That's where to look for a man's strength. In his wrists, his forearms. Would you like to have him hit you, Little Al?"

"I don't care." The huge man shook his head stubbornly. "I couldn't whip Drumgriffin."

"Just because you couldn't match the Irishman doesn't mean nobody else could."

"Listen." Little Al shoved his chair back so hard it fell over with a crash. He stood on his feet and pounded the

52

table. "I've been in every saloon from Frisco to New York. I've fought more monkeys than. . . ."

"All right, all right. So you licked every man from here to Timbuktu at rough-and-tumble, and you still couldn't lick Drumgriffin. We all believe you. Sit down." Poker had not raised his voice, but it stopped the man. Little Al towered above the table, frowning at the gambler, beefy jowls working. Finally, puzzled anger in his eyes, he turned, righting the chair, lowering his bulk onto it. "Maybe our friend here did catch Drumgriffin off guard," Poker said.

"Yeah." Little Al brightened. Some of his hearty humor returned. "That's what I'm sayin'."

"It doesn't matter," Poker continued. He was looking at Hagar with narrowed, studying eyes. "Ten thousand dollars," he said softly. "That's a lot of money."

"You must have an ear to the ground," Hagar said.

"I know about everything that goes on in War Bonnet, Hagar. Ever hear of Muley Banning? Bob Cherington?"

"No."

"Two of the War Bonnet cattlemen, Hagar. They were in the Pioneer House when Nicholet got back last night. He told them the figure you had proposed. Naturally it got around town pretty soon." He slipped a fat wallet from his coat and placed it on the table. "Ten thousand, cash. Have you got the papers?"

Hagar stared at the wallet. "You move fast."

"Are you stalling?"

"Did you think I'd have the papers on me?" Hagar asked.

"I didn't take you for a fool. But surely you can put your hands on them soon enough."

"Take me about half an hour."

"Good. Then we can discuss the other consideration."

"Is there another?"

Poker slipped the snub-nosed house gun from under his coat. "You didn't think I'd let you go without at least one round, did you?"

Little Al leaned forward. "Poker, don't be a fool. He's going to sell. The Quarter's ours. Don't take a chance like that now. You might be throwing the whole thing away."

"But look at what I'm gaining. What's the Bloody Quarter compared with it? If I could gain control of the whole world, I'd still stake it on one round of Russian poker." He snapped out the cylinder and spilled five .41-caliber shells into his hand. He thumbed one back into the cylinder, closed it, spun it. "Hagar?" he asked.

Hagar found himself staring at the gun. "Do you think I'm a fool?"

"What's the difference?" Poker said. "In effect, you've been staking your life on this thing ever since you got hold of the Bloody Quarter. Drumgriffin was pretty close to killing you last night. If you were willing to risk that, you should be willing to do this. Just one round, Hagar. It's all I ask."

"Boss, please . . . !"

"Shut up, Al. I haven't found a chance like this in months. Don't you see how we have him? He's gone too far for that ten thousand to back out now. He's already risked his life. The odds weren't even as good then. Four to one, Hagar. Where could you find better odds?"

Poker spun the cylinder again. The clicking sounded like a staccato roll of drums in the silent room.

Little Al was staring at the gun helplessly, a mesmerized look in his eyes. "He's crazy, when he gets going like this," he said. His voice sounded hollow. His lips were slack. "I saw him go fifteen rounds once with a boatman in Saint Looey. I thought I'd go off my nut, waiting for that thing to fire. I went on a three-day bat, when it was over. They had to scrape the boatman's brains off the ceiling."

"I'll go first, if you want, Hagar." Poker held the gun up to his head. The sweat was making his sallow forehead gleam now. His pupils were pinpoints of ecstasy. "A courtesy," he said.

"Boss," whimpered Little Al. "Please. I've watched you a hundred times. But not now. It's in our hands. Listen." He clutched Poker's arm. "I'll go with you myself . . . after he signs the deed over. I'll go with you out front, where everybody can see. . . ."

The *click* stopped him. Hagar felt his whole body jerk. Poker let the gun remain against his head an instant afterward, finger squeezed tightly against the trigger. Then the intense focus left the pupils of his eyes. They took on a glazed look. A little muscle fluttered in his cheek. He put the gun on the table. There was something spent about the breath that left him. He stared at Hagar, waiting.

"Your turn," he said finally. "I won't buy without it."

Hagar stared at him, seeing the crazy streak in his eyes, realizing he meant it. Then he found his eyes dropping to the gun. Was it worth it? What a crazy thought! He'd be a fool to even consider it. He found himself thinking of holding the gun to his head. Of pulling the trigger.

"Look at him," Poker said. His voice had a pinched sound. "It's getting him, Little Al. Have we found one of the true grit at last? There are so few left. What better odds could you ask, Hagar? What higher stakes? You've been speculating all your life. Aren't you tired of the penny-ante games? Is there really any kick left? Compare it with this. You don't know how it feels, Hagar. It's the kind of thrill you can't get anywhere else. A woman is nothing beside it. All of life is nothing. . . ."

He trailed off, eyes fixed on Hagar. *Just one time*. Hagar found it going through his head. *Just pick up the gun and spin it. Just squeeze it once. For ten thousand dollars. You've come this far. You won't get it any other way. Just one time.*

His head jerked up as he realized how deeply he had been sucked in. He stared at the fixed fascination of Poker's eyes, at the bucolic waiting in Little Al's face. He spoke, and he hardly recognized his own voice, it was so strained.

"Think I'd let you rope me into a sucker game like this?"

"It's no sucker game!"

The words left Poker in a shrill, womanish cry, bringing him against the table, gripping its edge with both hands. His face had a whipped look.

Little Al straightened sharply and grabbed his arm. "You shouldn't have said that," he told Hagar. "It's one thing he can't stand. This game ain't rigged. He's always played it straight."

It took a long time for Poker to settle back. The breath left him finally with a thin, hissing sound. His chin sank against his chest, and he spoke in a dead, mechanical way. "I won't buy without it."

"Then you won't buy."

The little muscle fluttered in Poker's cheek again. "There are twenty-six saloons in War Bonnet, Hagar. That's a pretty big combination to buck."

"As big as Ed Garland?" Hagar asked. He stood up. "I won't play the game, Poker. If you want to buy the quarter section, say so. If not, I'll leave."

"There are other ways."

"I'm tired of being threatened, Poker."

"That's your last word?"

"Is it yours?"

"It is."

Hagar turned toward the door. But he didn't think they would let it end so simply, and he wheeled right back. Poker was grabbing for the gun, and Little Al was jumping around the table at Hagar.

Hagar took one lunging step back to the table, caught it beneath the edge, and heaved. It went over on Poker just as he lifted the gun. He fell back with a sharp cry, the heavy deal table crashing down on top of him.

Little Al was a step from Hagar, when Hagar wheeled and jumped back from his rush. Hagar stumbled into one of the chairs still upright and almost fell. He jumped aside, caught its back, swung it high. Little Al was lunging in so hard he could not stop. One of the legs caught him in the eye, driving deep. He screamed and reeled back and doubled over with the pain, clapping both hands to his eye.

Hagar dropped the chair and whirled to tear the door open. The men about the faro layouts, the customers at the bar were all turned around toward number four. One of the barmen was just coming from behind the bar, wielding a wicked-looking shillelagh.

"Tanglefoot!" shouted Poker from the room behind Hagar. "Stop him, stop Hagar!"

"OK, OK," shouted the barman, waving the shills and dealers away from their layouts. A banker rose from a two-card box, pulling a house gun, and a couple of shills broke through the thin crowd at the faro layout. Hagar had his gun out, but he didn't want to use it in such a crowd. He dodged past Tanglefoot, but a shill came in from one side, catching at his right arm. He jerked free, whipping at the shill with his gun.

He knocked the man back, but Tanglefoot closed in from behind. Hagar heard the grunt and tried to wheel, but he got only far enough around to see the shillelagh coming down.

It made a blinding flash of pain in his head. He felt himself knocked aside, into the banker with the house gun. He dropped his own weapon and caught the man around the waist to keep from falling. He heard the shuffle of feet behind him and another grunt, and feebly tried to throw himself aside from Tanglefoot's second blow. He knew, in his pain, that he could not.

Then the shot smashed through the room.

It seemed to cut off all the noise, the shouting, the wild shuffling of feet. Hagar shoved himself free of the banker, surprised that the man was not whipping at him with the gun. Blinking, he turned to see the static poses of the customers at the bar, their open mouths, their wide eyes. Tanglefoot stood directly before him, staring blankly at the shillelagh in his hand. He was holding only half of it. The other half lay on the floor at his feet. It took Hagar a moment to realize the bullet must have broken it. Finally he looked across the room to the stove. The man in the rusty black suit was faced his way now. The cheroot was still tilted upward in his mouth. There was a smoking six-shooter in his hand.

"I don't like to see the odds stacked so high against anybody," he drawled. "Let's allow the gentleman to go on out."

Hagar gazed at him a moment longer, waiting for some break in the blank face, some recognition. But Missouri Carnes stared at him emptily, as if looking at a perfect stranger. Hagar grinned thinly.

"Thanks, stranger," he said.

Missouri did not even dip his head. Hagar bent to pick up his gun and turned to walk outside. He stopped a moment on the boardwalk, with the batwings screeching back and forth behind him. A new note had entered the noise of the town. A rider spurred his horse hard down toward a knot of people at the sheriff's office, and Hagar could see them unloading a body from a horse down there. The planks rattled beneath hurried feet from his left, and, before he could turn, someone caught his arm.

In impulsive reaction, he tore free, lifting the gun. But it was Napoleón Nicholet.

"Don't go down to your horse," the lawyer said quickly. "They're already coming to get it. My wagon's around in the alley. You've got to leave town as quickly as you can."

"Why?"

Nicholet waved toward the sheriff's office. "They've just brought in Carter John's body. Word is out about the tangle you had with him at the stage station . . . how you followed him on north. Ed Garland's already sworn out a warrant for your arrest on the charge of murder."

Chapter Six

Gathering dusk turned the mountains to billowing smoke that seemed to roll away on every side, fold upon fold, until it faded at last into the darkening sky. Somewhere in the cluster of juniper covering the footslopes a grackle was chattering sleepily. A growing spring breeze carried the rich tang of earth and drying grass to Hagar, as he guided his plodding team down the grade toward the dim spread of the flats below. He had not taken the Texas Trail south through the Laramies, but had followed a side route, and now he slumped wearily in the seat, the whip nodding in its socket beside him.

He was rattling across a dry streambed, when the sound came from behind him, dim and barely audible beneath the creak of axles and clatter of boards in the wagon. Hagar tugged at the scarred butt of his gun to loosen the weapon in its holster, and drew his team up on the far bank, turning in the seat.

It was one rider on a dusty chestnut with dappling across its chest that gave it the look of a roan. He came forward at a steady trot until he struck the dry bed, then pulled the horse up, walking it across the rocky bottom. He drew the animal up beside the buckboard. Hagar watched without speaking while the man stepped from the saddle onto the seat, hitching the horse's reins to the brake handle.

"Took your time about catching up with me, Missouri," said Hagar.

"They got a posse out after you, Paul. I didn't want to meet you till we could be alone," said Missouri. "I still don't know whether you've given them the slip or not."

"You don't want them to know we're acquainted?"

"It would be easier for me," said Missouri. "I had a talk with the boys in Little Al's after you left. They think I'm just an itinerant grub-line rider with a yen for seeing odds more even than they were in that fight."

Hagar clucked at his horses, and the two men jerked backward as the team lurched into motion. When they were rolling, he looked at the man beside him. There was a droll cynicism in Missouri Carnes's long, horse face, but there was humor in the crinkling around his sharp, blue eyes. He was as tall as Hagar but much narrower through the shoulders, a slight stoop giving him a look of sly indolence.

"You damn' old coyote," Hagar grinned. "How is it you always show up just in time to save my hide?"

"Maybe because there hasn't been one day in your life you didn't invite somebody to nail that hide on the wall." Missouri chuckled. He leaned back, drawing a deep breath. "Cheryl probably told you . . . I'm working for the railroad. Heard about you signing on the Bloody Quarter. About Garland bracing you at the shack. Figured you'd be in for Poker's bid today. Figured you might need a hand, if things got rough."

"I owe you a beer."

"We're even. I never bought you one for the Mexican you pulled off my back in Santa Fé."

The road wound down through scattered mats of timber. The wagon rattled and creaked over the rough spots. A stream chuckled softly from beyond a dark stretch of spruce.

"I'm sort of an advance man, Paul," Missouri said. "War Bonnet's present state of politics isn't healthy for my railroad. They were one of the groups instrumental in having old Albany County divided in half. They wanted Ed Garland's power broken up here."

"He's fighting the railroad?"

"In a sense," Missouri said. "He has a lobby in the state legislature that has got the shipping rates at Laramie to a ridiculously low point. The railroad's been taking a loss on every head of beef that's shipped out of Laramie. They've got to keep handling the beef or lose the other business."

"So they're interested in getting a shipping point that is not under Garland's domination."

"That's right," Missouri said. "War Bonnet is that point. The cattlemen around here would welcome it. Their cattle drop an average of ten pounds on the drive to Laramie. What they make up in low shipping rates, they lose in weight."

Hagar looked at the man. "You're saying the railroad doesn't want Garland to get hold of the Bloody Quarter."

Missouri grinned. "Whoever owns the Bloody Quarter owns War Bonnet. If Garland owned War Bonnet, he'd be as strong in Converse County as he is in Albany."

"Who are you backing, then?"

"Not the gamblers," Missouri said. "They always look for a big, quick profit, and they'd put as big a squeeze on us as Garland."

"All that's left is the ranchers."

Missouri shook his head. "Individually, they're too small. They'd be strong enough, if they stuck together, but they're always fighting among themselves. They'd be a poor bet."

"Who else is there?"

"You."

Hagar felt himself straightening, turning, staring in surprise at the man. "You must be joking, Missouri."

"I'm not. You're strong enough to do it. If you hung onto

the Bloody Quarter and guaranteed the ranchers passage over it to their high graze, it would give them something to rally around. All they need is a leader. But it couldn't be just a strong man. It would have to be a man who had in his hands something that would give him the power to control this situation. Something like the Bloody Quarter. The combination fits you like a kid glove."

Hagar shook his head. "Whoever holds that land is a target, Missouri. I'm not setting myself up for any clay pigeon."

"You already have," Missouri said. "And you've proved you could stick it. The railroad would back you, Paul. That means men and money. They'd help you pull the ranchers together till they were strong enough to buck both Garland and the gamblers. And I'm sure the railroad would make some financial arrangements with you on an annual basis for keeping the Quarter under wraps. You could develop the land, Paul. Add to it. You'd have something big, something bigger than you've dreamed."

For a moment, the possibilities stirred a dormant excitement in Hagar. Perhaps they touched his old speculative impulses. Or perhaps they were reaching something even deeper than that. Then he settled back on the seat.

"How could I give you my word I'd stay, Missouri? You know me."

Missouri pursed his lips meditatively. "A man can change, Paul."

"Do you really think so?"

"If the reason is big enough."

"That's the point. Your proposition reaches me. But I'm not even sure myself how long it would last. I might start getting restless next month."

"I'm not talking about the Bloody Quarter, Paul. Land

63

can mean a lot to a man. But it takes something else."

Hagar gave the man an oblique glance. "You talking about Cheryl?"

"She isn't married to Drumgriffin yet."

"Might as well be."

"How do you know?" Missouri said. "Cheryl sees you ride in here on a big wind, as always. Sees you immediately kick up the biggest ruckus War Bonnet has yet to see. As always. Sees you right off gambling on the main chance, going to make a killing, going to hit the trail with your loot. How else could she react?"

"I'm not blaming her."

"What if you stuck, Paul? I'd bet my new Stetson Drumgriffin wouldn't be on the inside track then."

"You know how many times I've tried."

"You were younger then. You've had a few things knocked into your head since. You could do it, Paul. You never had a better chance. Just show Cheryl. . . ."

Hagar shook his head. "I know what's in her mind. She was never like this before, never so sure. She'd always give me another chance. Now she knows exactly where she stands. She knows what she wants. It's not me."

They rolled off the road into the rocky ford of the creek, water dripping from the spokes, iron tires clanging against the boulders. Missouri was studying Hagar narrowly. He started to speak.

"Paul. . . ."

The shot blotted out his words. Before its deafening crash was dead, the horses bolted headlong out of the ford, screaming in fright. Hagar was fighting a set of taut reins that leaped and jerked like angry snakes in his hands. The wagon caromed off a tree, and he tried to avoid the next one by reining. The maddened beasts answered the pull by whirling completely about, ramming into one another, and crashing against a cottonwood as they lunged back toward the water. The wild turn had tilted the wagon. Hagar fought to balance it back with his weight. He felt the bed go beyond its center of gravity.

"Jump!" he shouted. He felt the seat rebound as the other man kicked free, then the wagon was going over, and Hagar let go the reins and threw himself into the echoing darkness.

The shock of striking stunned him. He was dimly aware of rolling through the crackling resilience of leaves and over the gritty softness of sand. A boulder thrust its smooth rondure into his back. Then the abrupt, icy clutch of water revived him with the spasmodic force of a blow. He floundered to his feet in the rocky shallows, hearing the insane screaming of the horses and the wild smashing of the buckboard as the horses fought to run with it upset like that. With all this racket, he hardly heard the next shot. The high whine of the bullet penetrated his consciousness, and he cringed instinctively. The bullet made a sharp splatter into the water at one side. Hagar threw himself down once more. He realized the moon had risen from behind the Laramies, and he was illuminated in a yellow light drifting down through the trees. The cottonwoods were beginning to shed their white tufts, and they bobbed on the water like lily pads, spreading softly away from the passage of Hagar's body as he crawled across a myriad of the round rock faces, seeking the shelter of a cutbank higher up.

The horses had finally broken free of their harness and were galloping off through the grove of trees. Hagar reached the cutbank in the silence that had dropped with a startling abruptness. It was a long time before any sound came to him. He did not think he could stand the icy water any longer, when at last he heard the rattle of chokeberry from somewhere up the slope. He took his mashed hat off his head and raised up till one eye was over the bank. The movement among the trees up there was barely discernible. Then a shadowy figure moved into one of the dappled pools of moonlight beneath the trees, coming hesitantly toward the ford.

Hagar's first impulse was to fire. He snaked his wet Remington from its holster, shifting it into position. But the distance was too far for any accuracy with a six-shooter.

He lay there, tense and shivering, watching the unrecognizable figure move like a black shadow through intermittent light and darkness. There was something familiar about the shape, the walk. It was too far away to place clearly.

Whoever it was stopped finally within the trees overlooking the portion of the stream farther down, where the buckboard lay on its side in the water. The figure remained there for a long time, still too far for an accurate shot, and the soft riffle of water about the overturned wagon was the only sound. Then the shadowy form turned and leaned forward slightly to move back upgrade.

Hagar wanted to follow. But he couldn't leave without being sure of Missouri. He crawled down to where they had jumped from the wagon. He found a torn chokeberry patch where Missouri must have hit. There was no sign of blood anywhere. Missouri had not been shot, then. And if he had been knocked out in the jump, he would still be here.

At last Hagar found the marks of Missouri's boots in soft, black soil, leading westward along the stream. The man had gone off on some tangent that only he could explain. It was typical of Missouri. It left Hagar's mind easy about the man. He had every confidence that Missouri could take care of himself, and, since the direction of the man's trail would take Hagar away from the figure he had seen, he forgot about Missouri and turned back upslope.

He took advantage of the trees, working upward swiftly, flitting through the resinous scent cast off by a stand of spring poplars. At last, chest heaving from the forced climb, he caught sight of the figure again, silhouetted on the ridge. He reached the ridge and kept from being skylighted himself by crouching in a nest of craggy rocks. Below him, in a little park, the figure was mounting a horse.

Still too deep in the shadows to be recognized, the rider turned down off the crest. Hagar followed, teeth chattering, sodden clothes crawling against his back. From this height he could see the road he had taken southward from War Bonnet in the wagon. It appeared intermittently from the dark stands of timber, like the transient flash of a silver ribbon. A second road forked from it to run westward between this ridge and the next.

The horsebacker led Hagar down to this side road and turned west. It was grass-grown, unmarked by recent use. There was a slight uphill grade to this trace, leading back into the depths of the valley, and, although the rider never lifted the animal out of that walk, Hagar was breathing heavily when he finally saw the cessation of movement ahead. There was the creak of saddle leather. The horse sighed heavily, and then was silent.

Hagar moved forward cautiously until he could see the animal. They stood at the fringe of a thick stand of Douglas fir, looking down an abrupt drop of the climbing valley floor into an open park. A house and outbuildings sprawled in silence at the bottom of this park, lifting their lightless shapes mordantly against the night.

It was hard to tell the barn from the house. They both had the same steep hip roof and stood about the same size.

Then Hagar caught the pattern of corrals about the far structure. The rider was leading the horse down through the open meadow now, finally stopping by the pens. Hagar could barely make out the movement of the figure near the horse, loosening the cinch. He moved across the top of the park till he found a line of firs he could shift down through, passing the corrals and going on till he could see the front of the barn.

The whole spread was in a bad state of disrepair. The windows of the house were boarded up, the corrals falling apart. With the barn between him and the figure at the corral, Hagar moved into the open, crossing to the barn. The huge front door was sagging open, with a shadowy hint of empty stalls and hayracks within. He walked carefully to the corner. From behind the wreck of a rusting plow he could see the figure again. Hagar was close enough to recognize the man now. It was Patrick Drumgriffin.

Chapter Seven

Hagar's first impulse was to step out, to challenge the man, but he suppressed it and remained hidden. Why had Drumgriffin come here? To meet someone?

The horse stamped frettingly. The Irishman lit a cigarette and smoked it down. Wet to the bone, Hagar had a dozen impulses to sneeze and fought them with a finger against his upper lip. Then the Irishman turned, looking upslope. He dropped the cigarette and ground it out. Another rider appeared in the moonlight. A woman, sitting sidesaddle. Cheryl Bannister.

The breath blocked up in Hagar. He stared at her as she came closer, approaching the pens from a direction that kept Hagar hidden to her. She reached Drumgriffin and swung down into his arms. Their figures blended into one. Hagar felt unreasoning anger fill him, raw and savage. It required an effort to remain still. There was a long silence, a rustling of clothing, a raggedly indrawn breath.

"You don't know how crazy I've been to do that these last days," Drumgriffin said.

"Why didn't you stop in at the Pioneer House?" she said. "You were in town today."

"I couldn't. Garland's kept me on the run. He doesn't want me to see you now. He's heard that you knew Hagar before, in Denver, and he's afraid you're working with Hagar on this deal. That's why I sent that note to meet me here. I had to see you, Cheryl."

"Are you that afraid of Garland, Pat? That you have to

sneak around behind barns to meet me?"

"It's not a matter of being afraid," he said roughly. "I don't want you sucked into this, Cheryl. If Garland got the idea you were working against him, he could ruin your business in War Bonnet."

"Pat." Her voice cut him off. "What was that wrecked wagon down at the crossing? I passed it coming in."

"I think somebody cut loose at Hagar," Drumgriffin said. "He lit out of town in Nicholet's rig. The sheriff got up a posse to follow. I think Hagar lost them, when he cut off the Texas Trail at Crow Notch. They were going straight on down the Texas, last I heard."

"But nobody was around the wagon!" There was a sharp fear in her voice. "Pat, what do you suppose . . . ?"

"I imagine Hagar got away, if that's what's worrying you."

"Pat . . . did you . . . did you . . . ?"

"Did I bushwhack Hagar?" There was a sudden flatness to Drumgriffin's voice. "What if I did?"

"Pat, you wouldn't!"

"Garland's right." Drumgriffin grabbed her shoulders. "There *is* something between you and that drifter. What did he mean to you in Denver, Cheryl?"

"You're hurting me, Pat."

He held her a moment longer, staring at her. Then he let her go, the breath leaving him with a guttural sound. Finally he said: "Do you really think that's the way I operate, Cheryl?"

She seemed to be studying his face. "I don't want to, Pat. But if you didn't bushwhack Paul Hagar, who did?"

"I don't particularly care. Maybe some of Poker's crowd. What I want to know is . . . what was between you and him?"

"It's over, Pat." Her voice had a tired sound. "Whatever was between Paul Hagar and me is over. Can't you let it go at that?"

He stared at her a long time. "I guess I'll have to," he said.

She came close to him again. "It's what's between us that counts now, Pat. It will be spoiled unless you get out from under Garland. Can't you see what all this is leading up to?"

"I promised Garland I'd see this thing through before I quit. If I walked out on him now and he got control of Converse County anyway, he'd see that I'd never make a go of it here. You know him."

"That's the whole point," Cheryl said. "If he gets control up here, what good would it do to quit him? You'd be just as much under his thumb as if you were on his payroll. You'd be just another one of these small ranchers Garland would control, if he got the Quarter."

"No, I won't. Garland's agreed to let me use that pass no matter what pressure he has to bring against the other ranchers."

"Then you might as well stay with him. You'd be no more than Garland's errand boy moved up north."

"It's the deal I had to make, Cheryl. A man can't work for Ed Garland so long and just step out. A 'puncher, maybe, but not a man who's been on the inside of things like I have. We'd have to get clear out of the country. If we mean to stay here, we've got to make some compromise."

"Don't you see how you're playing right into Garland's hands? You know what a big fuss he made when you told him you were pulling out. You'll be tied to his apron strings as tightly as ever."

"No, I won't. I can't break away completely and keep

what I've set up. It'll have to come in a series of little breaks. This is just the first one."

"Oh, Pat! You'd be all alone up here. The ranchers would never have anything to do with you. They'd see you using that pass, when they couldn't. They'd know you were still with Garland. Quit now. Join them now."

"And get squeezed out for good when Garland gets the Quarter?"

"Perhaps Garland won't get the Quarter," Russian Poker said softly, from the inky shadows beyond the corral.

Both Drumgriffin and Cheryl whirled that way.

The gambler moved from beneath a line of cottonwoods just beyond the north fence of the pen. Moonlight glittered dully on the nickel-plated house gun in his hand.

"I didn't know you counted eavesdropping among your meager talents," Cheryl said thinly.

"I have no scruples," Poker said blandly. "You should know that by now. You picked a poor man to carry your note to Cheryl, Drumgriffin. He read what was in it and brought the news to me, after he'd delivered it to her. I have a standing offer among the town loafers for items of that sort. I've long wondered just how much business you mixed with the pleasure of your meetings. You disappoint me. I thought you'd be hatching some dark plot to keep the Syndicate from gaining control of the Quarter."

Drumgriffin's voice was rough with anger. "How long you been here?"

"I saw you both come in."

"Maybe you came in across Cotton Creek ford."

"That's the only way in, from War Bonnet," Poker said. "If you're thinking I bushwhacked Hagar, however, you're mistaken. I was just topping the ridge, when it happened. I saw who did it."

"Who?" Drumgriffin asked sharply.

Poker idly spun the cylinder of his gun with a thumb. "None of Garland's men. None of my men. Surely none of the ranchers' men. Here we've thought all along that this was a simple contest of power between the War Bonnet Syndicate and Ed Garland and the valley ranchers. Now we find there is a fourth party involved. A party willing to kill to win."

Drumgriffin's fists were tensely closed. "Who was it, Poker?"

"That knowledge would be valuable to you in more ways than one, wouldn't it?" Poker said. "Are you thinking you could use it to get out from under Garland? A club over his head, maybe? Or sell it to him . . . the price being your freedom?"

"Damn you, Poker, I'll. . . ."

"No, you won't." Poker's silken voice stopped Drumgriffin cold. He had the house gun pointed at the big man. "Just how badly do you want the name of the fourth party, Drumgriffin?"

"What are you saying?"

"Maybe I have a price, too."

"Name it."

Cheryl caught Drumgriffin's arm. "Pat, don't deal with him."

Drumgriffin half turned, shaking her off. "I've got to. Don't you see what this could mean? He's right. Garland has to know who that fourth party is. He might lose this whole thing, if he doesn't. Every move he made might be the wrong one. It would be a club over his head." He whirled back to Poker. "What's the price?"

Poker smiled. That strange, spasmodic smile. With a flirt of his wrist, he snapped out the cylinder, removing four bul-

lets from the five-shot house gun. Then he snapped the cylinder back in.

"Three rounds," he said. "Just three rounds."

Even in the treacherous moonlight, Hagar could see the
blood drain from Cheryl's face. "No." It left her in a lost,
sighing way. "Pat, no, don't be a fool."

"Are you crazy?" Drumgriffin asked.

"You know I am, when it comes to Russian poker," the
gambler said. "If I had a chance at a million dollars, I'd give
it up to play this game. I'd crawl from here to Frisco for one
round. I'd forgive any man my own murder, if he'd play."
Poker's eyes were beginning to glitter. "Come on, Drumgriffin. I'll settle for two rounds. Doesn't it reach you?
Nothing else touches it. Like drink. Like dope. Only a hundred times more. Once you get started, you can't stop." He
broke off, breathing swiftly, eyes shining.

Hagar stared at him, trying to reconcile this childish excitement with the man's usual wooden impassivity.

"Are you afraid?" Poker asked.

"I'm not afraid of any man or any thing in the world, and
you know it!" Drumgriffin roared.

"Pat!" cried the woman. "Don't let him goad you."

"Then why won't you do it?" Poker asked in a high voice.
He took a jerky step toward them. "Think what it could
mean. Getting out from Garland. I'll even settle for one
round. You're in a hole, Drumgriffin, and you won't get out
any other way. You'd always be tied to Garland's apron
strings. This could make the difference. Just one go, Pat,
just one second, and you'll have the world."

Drumgriffin stared at the man, a mingling of expressions
shuttling across his face. He took a deep breath. "Give me
the gun," he said.

"Pat," Cheryl said. "Pat, please . . . !"

Grinning fixedly, Poker walked toward the Irishman, holding out the gun, butt first. Hagar stepped around the corner, Remington in his hand.

"Stop right there, Poker. Drop that gun, or I'll cut you in two."

The gambler's whole body stiffened as he came to a halt. Both Cheryl and the Irishman wheeled sharply toward Hagar. Poker was holding his house gun by the barrel and could not possibly switch it in time. He let it drop from his hand.

"Paul," Cheryl said breathlessly. "Where . . . ?"

"I've been here all the time," Hagar said. "I trailed Drumgriffin in from the creek. Poker couldn't have got there in time to see who the bushwhacker was. If he'd been here before any of us arrived, he would have seen me coming down after you. And he obviously didn't even know I was here. He was just baiting up another customer for that game of his."

Drumgriffin turned back to the gambler, fists working. "Damn you, Poker, I ought to tear you apart."

The gambler had regained his composure. He shrugged, and his voice held a thin cynicism. "I told you, Drumgriffin. Once you get started, you can't stop."

The Irishman turned back to Hagar. "You're a funny bucko. After the way we came at you the other night, anybody else would have let me blow my brains out."

"You have a lot to learn about Paul," Cheryl said. She studied Hagar for a moment, biting her underlip, then looked at Poker. "You really don't know who tried to kill Paul?"

"No," Poker said.

"And there isn't really a fourth party?" Hagar asked.

"On the contrary," Poker said. "We all know the ranchers

75

wouldn't do it. They just don't work that way. I know I didn't do it. Drumgriffin would know, if Garland did it, and, if we are to believe Drumgriffin, Garland didn't. What does that leave us?"

Hagar stared at the man, frowning. "A very interesting complication," he said at last.

There was a soft sound from the far side of the pen. It drew Hagar's gaze.

"Wind coming up," Poker said.

Cheryl was looking behind Hagar. "Paul . . . !"

But he had heard it, too. The same kind of sound. Like the wind, yet not like the wind. And too late.

"Don't move, Hagar," Jack Willows said softly. "We're all around you. Drop your gun."

Hagar felt his fingers tighten around the butt of his Remington in reaction. Then he spread them, letting the gun fall. After that, somebody straightened up behind the fallen barricade of the far fence. Moonlight glittered against the star on his chest.

"All right, men," he said gruffly. "This is him."

There was more of the soft sound, and forms began to materialize from the timber. Jack Willows moved from behind the barn and into Hagar's vision. The tobacco made its inevitable bulge in his weather-textured cheek, warping his triumphant grin.

Hagar couldn't keep the anger from his voice. "You been out there all the time?"

"Just closed in," Willows said. "The bulk of the posse went on down the Texas Trail. Only a couple of men took this cutoff to check. We wouldn't have picked you up, if you hadn't wrecked the wagon at the ford. One of the men went back for the posse. When they hit the wreck, they spread out and started combing. I was the one that spotted you from the ridge, talking down here."

"Garland'll give you a medal," Hagar said thinly.

A pair of men, leading horses, had emerged from the cottonwoods behind Poker. The man with the sheriff's star joined them and came around the pen to Hagar. One of them was Ed Garland. His pale eyes gleamed as white, as chill as ice in the moonlight. They caught Drumgriffin in a brief, stabbing glance.

The Irishman started to lift his hand. "Ed. . . ."

"Shut up!" Garland's voice crackled like a whip. "You and I had our last words about Cheryl. If you've been cooking up a deal against me, I'll know it soon enough, and you know what will happen to you then."

Hagar saw little knots of muscle jump up along Drumgriffin's jaw, but Garland gave him no time to answer. Those pale eyes were on Hagar now. The grooves on either side of Garland's mouth had dug so deeply they looked like wounds. His voice changed, became thin, brittle.

"Carter John was very close to me," he said. "He was my only heir, and he was very close to me."

"I'm sorry for that," Hagar told him.

"Sorry!" Garland's voice broke. He started to take another step forward, and then stopped. His fists were clenched so tightly the tendons stood out in white ridges. "Give me five minutes alone with him, Steele," he said. There was a guttural tone to his voice now. "Just five minutes."

"You know we can't do it that way, Ed," the sheriff said.

"Then get it over with." The words seemed torn from Garland. He dropped his reins and made a jerky turn and paced across the grass. Then he stopped and turned back, his fists still clenched. "You're going to hang, Hagar. He was my nephew, and you're going to hang!"

"I didn't kill him, Garland," Hagar said.

"Steele!" Garland said hoarsely.

The lawman cleared his throat, brushing a finger across his walrus mustache. "I'm Sheriff Jeb Steele. By authority vested in me, I'm placing you under arrest for the murder of Carter John."

"The authority isn't vested in you," Hagar said. "You're out of your jurisdiction. This is Converse County."

"The boundary dispute's still going on," Garland said. His voice shook with rage. "Till it's settled, the sheriffs in either county have jurisdiction."

"Then why didn't you get the Converse sheriff? You came out of War Bonnet. You haven't got a Converse man in this posse. They're all E Bar G riders."

"Steele!" shouted Garland. "Put those cuffs on him!"

The rest of the posse had surrounded them now, half a dozen tall-hatted figures, holding Winchesters or six-shooters. Willows took a step nearer Hagar, lifting his gun higher. The handcuffs clanked as Steele unhooked them from his belt.

"Hold out your hands."

"Don't do it, Paul," Cheryl said.

With his hands half lifted, Hagar looked past Steele, past the 'punchers. In drawing closer, the men had all passed Cheryl. She had been but one pace from Poker's dropped house gun and had reached it before he had. It was a small gun, but it looked like a cannon in her slim hand. It was pointed at Steele.

"Don't be a fool," Garland said sharply. "You'll finish yourself in War Bonnet, if you do this."

He had started toward her. He stopped. She had switched the gun to him.

"War Bonnet isn't your town yet," she said. "And you're not taking Paul. I am."

Garland made a vicious gesture at the others. "Get her. She can't handle that thing. She's only a woman."

"I wouldn't make that mistake," Hagar said. "She can probably shoot a gun better than any of you."

"I should be able to," Cheryl said. "Paul Hagar taught me."

Chapter Eight

In the sheltered basins of the Laramies, where the snow piled so deep it did not melt all summer, the Engelmann's spruce crowded out the fir and lodgepole, standing ageless and benign in the somber shadows beneath high rock faces. Hagar had never been so high in these mountains before. In places there was an old logging road, then only a game trail, finally no trace at all to guide them, as they drove their nervous horses over bare rock sheeting or up gritty talus slopes.

They stopped on every ridge to study their back trail. But there was no sign of the posse. They had rounded up all the horses and had driven them a couple of miles before turning them loose. Hagar doubted if the men would be able to follow them under those circumstances. With the first pressure off, he asked Cheryl where she was taking him.

"Nicholet has a place," she said. "He had a note on it, and the man died. Not many people in War Bonnet know of it." She turned to him. "Paul . . . ?"

"I didn't kill Carter John, Cheryl, if that's what's on your mind," he said. He saw some of the tension die out of her eyes. Then he couldn't help chuckling. "You weren't sure. You didn't know yourself whether I'd done it. And still you pulled me out of that."

Her chin lifted angrily. "There's a difference between killing and murder, Paul. I know you didn't murder Carter John. And if you killed him, I was sure it happened under circumstances on which any court would free you. Any court except that in Laramie, at least. Garland has enough power in that town to hang you, if he ever got you down there."

"I'm just wondering how much of his grief was real."

"I don't think he has the capacity to care about anyone very deeply," she said. "I think it was more anger than grief. He must have gone to a lot of trouble over this plan . . . and then to have you wreck it in an instant."

"If Garland set it up so Carter John could sign on the Bloody Quarter before anybody found out the land was open, you'd think John would have been waiting in War Bonnet."

Cheryl shook her head. "The minute any man connected with Garland showed up, the whole town would have known something was ready to pop. Carter John had to wait till the last minute."

"Seems like longer than the last minute. The clerk had expected him that morning."

"Carter John was always irresponsible," she said. "He probably started out the night before. But if I know him, he had to stop in for just one drink before he left. One led to another, and he probably had to sleep it off."

"No wonder he was so touchy at Aspen Creek," Hagar said ruefully. "Riding a hangover, too. What about the rest of it? Is the land commissioner one of Garland's men, too?"

"I don't think so. He was down in Cheyenne about that squabble over the boundary. Garland probably pulled some strings to keep the squabble hot and prevent the commissioner from returning, then bribed the clerk up here not to put up the notices announcing the opening of the land."

"But why would Garland pick Carter John?"

"Garland owns too much land to be eligible for homesteading himself. So does Pat. He probably couldn't trust any of his hands with something so hot. The only one left was Carter John. The boy was Garland's heir, but he didn't own any property."

Hagar shook his head. "How unfortunate that such a beautiful plan had to hinge on such a weakling."

"Is it still only that to you, Paul? Just a plan? Just something to be manipulated for profit?"

Hagar sent her a sardonic glance. "Do you want me to join with the little ranchers, too?"

She flushed deeply. "That was unfair, Paul."

"As unfair as you're being with Drumgriffin?" he asked. "He's in a spot. If he quits Garland now, he'll never be finished fighting the man. But you want him to step out right away . . . want him to join the little ranchers, knowing yourself they aren't strong enough to stand against Garland or gain control up here."

"Paul!"

"It must be the way your mind works. You want me to sell to the ranchers. What good would that do, if they couldn't hold onto the Quarter?"

She turned to him, struggling against her anger with a set face. "Are you saying you'd sell to the ranchers, if you knew they could keep what they got?"

He settled a little in the saddle, staring at her. The question took him by surprise. He had been trying to show her the fallacy of her reasoning, and she had turned it on him.

Before he could recover, form his answer, she shook her head. "I thought so. You haven't changed. You're in it for the big strike, and that's all it means to you."

"Cheryl. . . ."

"Let's drop it, Paul. We have a lot of riding to do."

She turned to look ahead, anger hardening the line of

her cheek. He knew it would be useless to discuss it further, when she was in this mood.

They wore the night out till it became gray with coming dawn. They crossed countless ridges, threaded through endless cañons, splashed through the swift-running water of a dozen spring creeks. Finally they dropped down a slope where the thick strands of fir were blackened with old-man's beard, wended their way through aspens quivering in the breeze, and dropped off a sandy cutbank into the dry wash of a stream. They followed this up the cañon. It pinched down, choked up, till they were fighting their way through scrub growth and buckbrush. The cutbanks rose sheer above them, higher than their heads, and beyond that the ridges gnawed at a morning sky. Suddenly they broke from the choking growth into a glen where a shack and a pack-pole corral stood. The girl dismounted wearily, walked softly to the door, and shoved it open with her foot. It was slung on rawhide hinges and scraped across the puncheon floor protestingly.

Following her, Hagar saw one room with a plank table beneath the narrow, double-hung window and a pair of bunks across the rear wall.

"Little coffee left," she muttered, rummaging around on the shelf among the cartons and sacks. "Ought to be some tinned beef here somewhere. Even flour. Enough to last you a couple of days. Nicholet will be up as soon as he can. He's a good lawyer. He may be able to do something about that murder charge. Garland drummed it up pretty quick. There are probably holes in it."

He went to her, turning her around. "Cheryl, I'm sorry, if I said the wrong thing."

"Forget it, Paul. You're in a spot, too. It may squeeze you even tighter. I'll do what I can to help."

She did not move back. She continued to stare up at him, a strange darkness passing into her eyes. Her underlip ripened, trembled.

"In Denver," he said softly, "I would have kissed you at this point."

He saw tears well into her eyes. She wheeled sharply. "Paul . . . ," she said, in a choked voice. Then she walked to the door and stopped there a moment, shoulders pulled in. Finally she straightened up, speaking sharply. "I'll be going now. Wait for Nicholet, please. He's your only chance."

After she was gone, he unsaddled the black he had taken and turned it into the small corral. Then he hiked into the upper end of the gorge, where it ran against the mountain, to find water. There was a feeble spring there, and he filled the bucket he had found at the building. He filled the coffee pot and an old pail by the door before he watered the horse. There was an old six-plate stove in one corner and a stack of rotting wood someone had cut long ago. The flour on top of the sack was pocked with mold, but farther down it was good enough for biscuits. After eating, Hagar got the blankets and went out, closing the door. He moved into the scrub oak and made his bed where he would be within sight of the cabin, yet invisible from there. Cheryl had said few people knew about this place, but he was taking no chance.

Sleep should have come swiftly. He was dead tired from the all-night ride. But sleep would not come. There were too many issues at work in his mind. He found himself thinking of the shooting at the creek. Could it really have been a fourth party? And if so, what was *his* stake?

Or had Poker merely been throwing up a smoke screen? That was a more logical conclusion. Yet the other possibility kept nagging Hagar.

And then the picture of Cheryl in Drumgriffin's arms

came to haunt him. It was like scraping at a wound. He tried to blot it out with the other considerations. Was Cheryl right? Would he refuse to sell to the ranchers even if he knew they could hold the Quarter? He shook his head. It was unlikely he'd ever have to face the possibility. From what he had heard, they would never gain the strength for that. The money was the only consideration, then. If they could raise the ten thousand, he'd sell to them. Finally he drifted into a troubled sleep.

He spent the next day restlessly scouting the ridges above the shack, and at night he again placed his blankets out in the scrub oak.

He did not know how long he had been asleep. Perhaps it was the light of the rising moon first touching his face. Or some unconscious awareness in him discerning a small sound that his conscious perception would have missed. He found himself awake, staring up at the dark foliage of the scrubby trees above him. He lifted his head till he could see the shack. Then he moved his hand till it lay on the gun beside him. He remained motionless for a long time before the figure came from the trees beyond the shack. Hagar got the impression that the man had waited there during that interval, watching the building. He carried a short-barreled gun of some sort. He moved up to the shack and stood in the shadow of the wall for another long space. Finally he began to shove the door open on its rawhide hinges, slowly, painfully, halting every inch or so. Then he stepped inside.

Hagar rolled from the blankets and moved toward the shack from its side wall, invisible from the doorway. An owl began to hoot from the juniper on the higher slope. Listening through the cracks in the wall, Hagar could hear no sound from within. A clever man would be waiting for his eyes to accustom themselves to the darkness. After a time there was a soft shift across the floor.

Hagar was standing at the corner of the shack, when the figure stepped out again, holding the short-barreled gun out in front, looking from side to side in a swift, desperate way.

"I've got a gun on you," Hagar said. "Don't turn around."

The man stiffened, then a shaky chuckle escaped him. "Hagar?" he said.

Hagar recognized the voice, although the figure was still only a blot to him in the inky shadows. He lowered his gun, grinning ruefully, and stepped around the corner. "What in hell were you playing cowboys and Indians for, Nicholet?" he asked.

The lawyer slipped his gun under his coat. "Cheryl told me you were here. When I didn't see your horse in the corral, I thought something had happened. I couldn't afford to take any chances, either." Nicholet's mild smile was dimly visible to Hagar. "You'll have to take a chance now, Paul. You'll have to put yourself in my hands, if you want to escape this murder charge. I've been setting it all up. Obviously we can't let them take you to Laramie for the trial. That's Garland's town. He wants you down there the worst way. You can see the deal he would make then. Your freedom for the deed to the Bloody Quarter. If you wouldn't do it, he'd see that you were hanged."

"I figured that might be in his mind."

"Sheriff Steele is waiting to nab you the minute you show. That's why we've got to time our appearance perfectly. I've found the hole in their setup. Do you remember where Carter John was murdered?"

"A valley, a creek, that's all I remember."

"Big Squaw Valley."

"The one in the boundary dispute?"

"That's it. Big Squaw's got some of the best graze, the best water in the state. The ranchers of both counties are fighting over it. Albany County wants the line drawn along the north ridge. Converse wants it along the south. Last month Garland brought criminal suit against a rancher in that strip. The court ruled that neither county could have jurisdiction over suits arising in the disputed area. Using that as a precedent, I appealed directly to the Attorney General's office at Cheyenne. They said any duly appointed officer of the law had authority to arrest you. But since the murder was committed in the disputed strip, the trial itself would necessarily come under state jurisdiction. Clear so far?"

"Sounds logical."

"A circuit court judge reaches War Bonnet tomorrow. He'll sit there a week. I've pulled some strings to have your case the first on the docket. It will be merely the arraignment at first, no jury or anything. The town marshal will be waiting at the edge of War Bonnet to put you under arrest so Sheriff Steele won't get you."

Hagar could not help grinning. "You really pulled a deal, didn't you?"

Nicholet studied him carefully. "Don't you trust me?"

"It's not that so much. But once in the hands of the law, I'm a dead duck, if something slips up. Out here I'm still free, at least."

"You'd have to leave the state to escape, Hagar. You'd have to run the rest of your life, if you had that murder charge hanging over your head."

Hagar nodded, realizing how true that was. "What happens when we see the judge?"

"A lot of legal maneuvering that would be hard to explain here. But I'm sure I can free you. I've been working night and day to set it up."

"And what will you get out of it?"

The mild smile crossed Nicholet's face again. "You're a realist."

"Nobody would do this for free. That's nothing against you. What do you want? The promise that I'll sell to the ranchers?"

"If they meet your terms?" Nicholet asked.

"Ten thousand?"

"Ten thousand."

"What brought them around?" Hagar asked.

"Does that matter? If you'll sell, they'll buy. Have you got the deed with you?"

"No."

"Don't tell me you entrusted it to someone else. Cheryl?"

"No."

"Where is it, then, Hagar? You'll have to sign the papers over."

"You're a little eager, aren't you?"

The lawyer settled back, flushing. Then he smiled ruefully. "You'd trust me with your life, but not with a little piece of paper."

"That's how it is," Hagar grinned. "Shall we go to War Bonnet?"

Chapter Nine

Maybe it was the silence. It had been noisy, the first time Hagar had entered War Bonnet—the overwhelming surf of sound so characteristic of a boom town. But now there was only silence. There were little knots of men clustered all along the boardwalk, looking up and down the street. Most of the traffic was pulled up to the curbs, heavy Murphy wagons piled high with hay, freight wagons in a line before Whitworth's Feed, gigs and spring buggies and buckboards and a hundred horses crowding the racks before the other buildings.

Nicholet and Hagar pulled to a halt in the dense timber shrouding the northern slopes that overlooked the town. The lawyer squinted watery eyes to read the brands on a group of horses hitched before a saloon at the north end of the street.

"E Bar G," he muttered. "They were there, when I left. It's right across from the building Fogerty's using as a court. Garland must figure we mean to pull something soon. He's probably got Sheriff Steele waiting to nab you the minute you show. Marshal Carey has planted his three deputies up near the north end of town to decoy Steele and Garland that way. We'll come down Cimarron Alley, near the south end. Carey's waiting in a shack there."

They left their horses in the trees and used what cover they could to work down the slope. Finally they reached the outlying tarpaper shacks and rotting log cabins of the first settlers. Cimarron Alley began here, winding a crooked way down into the south end of Center Street. A man stepped from the open door of a cabin with a swift, purposeful stride. He was short and square with a black, spade beard and burning, black eyes beneath his heavy brow. There was a silver star on the left breast of his greasy, hickory jacket, and he carried a Greener with its double barrels sawed off short.

"Hagar," said Nicholet, "this is Marshal Chip Carey."

Marshal Carey spoke in clipped tones. "Garland's got men in that alley behind the judge's chambers as well as out on Center."

"We'd better move down Center, then," Nicholet said. "It's out in the open."

"That's it," Carey said. "They could block us off too easy in the alley. I'll have to take your gun, Hagar. I'm placing you under arrest."

Hagar handed over his Remington. The three of them then went on down Cimarron Alley until they reached the main street. Here they turned north.

The cottony silence suddenly broke. All along the walk, the knots of men turned to stare, and the voices beat up in a muffled roar. The boardwalk cleared before them as they moved northward. In the doorway of Little Al's, Hagar saw Russian Poker's slim figure and the man in the calico vest who had been planted to file on the Quarter. Then, a block up, the batwings of a second saloon slapped open, and Sheriff Steele stepped out. He glanced behind him and ran an indecisive finger across his walrus mustache.

A cluster of E Bar G riders filled the door and spilled onto the boardwalk, forcing the sheriff farther toward the curb. Then Ed Garland and Jack Willows stepped from the mouth of an alley across the street, the surprise plain in their faces, as they stared down Center at the oncoming trio.

Garland's voice rose bitterly over the other hubbub. "Steele!"

The tall sheriff turned sharply toward Garland, then stepped down off the curb, and started quartering toward the middle of the street. Still half a block from him, Hagar was searching the knots of men along the boardwalk for Drumgriffin.

"Where's the Irishman?" he asked tensely.

"He and Garland had a squabble over Cheryl Bannister, I understand," Chip Carey said. "Garland thinks Drumgriffin has been making some kind of deal with her behind his back. Drumgriffin's probably in some saloon, drinking it off."

"Or drinking off his fight with Cheryl," Nicholet said.

"Fight?" Hagar said.

"Over you," Nicholet said. "Right in the lobby of the Pioneer House. I was eating dinner at the time. Drumgriffin claimed she saved you because she was still in love with you. It really got hot. I've never seen Cheryl so mad. She ordered him out of the place." Nicholet looked at Hagar with twinkling eyes. "Funny part of it was, she never did deny that she was still in love with you."

Hagar sent him a sharp look.

Carey's voice came tersely. "No more talking now. Steele's here."

The sheriff had halted in the middle of the street, fifty feet ahead of them. "I want that man, Carey," he said.

Carey kept walking straight ahead without shifting the Greener from his elbow. "He's in my custody, Steele."

"You have no jurisdiction," said Steele. His voice sounded strident now. "I have the warrant originally sworn out for his arrest. I'm taking him."

"Not in my town," said Marshal Carey.

Garland did not shout, but his voice seemed to shake the whole row of buildings on that side. "Don't try to buck me, Carey. I'll have you removed from office so fast . . . !"

"My tenure of office doesn't depend on your dirty politics, Garland," interrupted Carey, in a lethal tone. "I was elected by the people of this town to maintain law and order within its limits. If you try to take Hagar from me by force, I'll construe it as a direct violation of the peace. I've used this shotgun before on violators. I'm perfectly capable of doing it again."

Walking between Carey and Nicholet, Hagar was swept with a wave of utter helplessness. Sweat had broken out on his palms, and he realized his fists were clenched. Their boots made a steady tattoo on the hard-packed earth.

"Steele," said Garland, "are you going to take that man or not?"

Carey walked right at Steele, lifting his shotgun till its muzzle was aimed at the man's belly. Steele's glance was fixed on that shotgun in the last instant. Then it fluttered, broke. With a helpless frustration in his seamed face, he stepped aside. They kept on walking at that steady pace, and he had to take a couple of long strides to catch up, paralleling them five feet from Carey's right elbow.

"Steele!" shouted Garland.

The sheriff's eyes were filled with a tortured expression as they swung to Garland. "Carey's right about jurisdiction, Ed. It's his town."

"The hell it is!" bellowed Garland. "Your county authority supersedes any jurisdiction he has here. You're through, if you don't take that man, Steele. You have every legal right, and you're through if you don't do it."

Steele started breaking inward, but Carey swung his shotgun toward the man. "I mean it about this Greener,

Steele. You don't have any authority in Converse."

They were almost at the end of the block now. Fifty feet ahead of them, Garland and Willows stood on the left side of the street. The half dozen E Bar G hands were walking up the right side, keeping even with Carey and Hagar and Nicholet. Garland stepped out toward the center, his face flushed with rage. As it if were a signal, the 'punchers began to fan out in front of the trio. Jack Willows moved to block the way, and another group of 'punchers spilled from the mouth of an alley beyond.

"Damn you, Steele!" Garland shouted. "If you won't do it, I'll do it myself. You have no right to that man, Carey. He's already been placed under arrest by the sheriff of Albany County." He broke into a hard walk toward Carey, followed by Willows. The 'punchers converged, their faces shining with sweat, their eyes glittering with tension.

Carey swung his shotgun from Steele to cover Garland, but the rancher did not stop coming forward. Only a few feet separated them now.

There was a furtive motion to Carey's left. The marshal tried to wheel, but Steele had jumped in too fast. The sheriff struck downward with his hand, knocking the muzzle of the shotgun toward the ground and coming heavily against Carey before the marshal could recover. Carey was knocked off balance, into Hagar.

At the same time, Garland and Willows jumped toward Hagar, drawing their guns, and there was a general rush among the 'punchers. Then the shot smashed out.

Hagar saw Garland's hat plucked from his head. Garland stopped as if he had run into a stone wall. He stood frozen in the street, staring at Nicholet. In the same instant, Hagar had stepped back to free himself of Carey, and the marshal had swung himself clear of Steele, jerking the shotgun up again. But he didn't need to use it. The 'punchers had stopped, and so had Jack Willows. It was like a static picture.

Some of them were staring at Garland's hat, in the street, with the bullet hole puncturing its crown. Some were staring at Garland. But most of them were staring at Nicholet.

Hagar saw that the lawyer held that little gun of his in his hand, with smoke wreathing from its muzzle.

A bland smile was on Nicholet's face. In the silence that had fallen, his voice held a quiet, conversational quality. "I could kill you with the next one, Garland. There are a hundred witnesses to the fact that you instigated the action, and that it was purely a matter of defending an unarmed man on my part. I've freed two clients on that plea. It's as good as self-defense."

Nicholet's innocuous eyes had taken on a milky light. Garland stared into them, with the blood slowly filling his face again, till it was ruddy with anger. His breathing made a stentorous sound in the painful silence.

Finally Nicholet said: "Step aside, now, Garland. We'll go on through."

Garland hesitated a moment longer. Hagar could see him trembling with frustrated rage. Then, his hands closed into fists, he stepped aside.

The voices of the crowd swelled into an awed murmuring. It was an eerie sound, sweeping along the street like the whisper of wind-blown leaves. It seemed to press against Hagar with a clammy weight as he walked the gauntlet of their eyes, between Nicholet and Carey. Garland and Willows and the 'punchers hung on their flanks like hungry wolves, but Carey kept swinging his shotgun, and the E Bar G men made no further attempt to get Hagar.

They reached the two-story building at Center and

Fourth. Carey took up his position at the door of the outside stairs, allowing Hagar and Nicholet to go in. Garland started to follow. Carey blocked the way with his Greener.

"Let them reach the chambers. Then you can go up. And only you."

"That was sharpshooting," Hagar told the lawyer as they climbed the stairs. "You can't convince me you haven't used that gun before."

Nicholet's smile was deprecating. "A pure accident."

"You're an old fox," Hagar grinned. "And I guess I owe you my life."

"If you continue to make it so embarrassing," Nicholet said, "I'll let them take you the next time."

They walked down the hall to the open door leading into the chambers. It was actually no more than a large double bedroom with a temporary rail across the middle. Judge Fogerty sat at a mahogany desk in the section behind the rail, a cold-eyed, snowy-haired man past fifty, wearing a black broadcloth and a string tie. A bailiff let Hagar and Nicholet through the gate. Fogerty nodded to the tall, stooped man standing before his desk.

"You know Lucas, Garland's lawyer."

Lucas removed pince-nez from a beak-like nose and nodded perfunctorily. Nicholet and Hagar nodded back. The hall outside echoed the impatient tramp of boots, and Garland stamped in. The bailiff let him through, and he took up his stand by Lucas, glaring at Hagar. Fogerty sorted through the pile of legal foolscap on his desk, finally waved his hand at a sheaf.

"These depositions from the station-keeper and the hostler at the Aspen Creek stage station, testifying that they saw Hagar fight with Carter John . . . that's the only evidence on which the warrant was sworn out?"

Lucas cleared his throat, adjusting his pince-nez. "You have another statement there . . . from the War Bonnet deputy. Hagar reported the killing to him."

"That doesn't do you much good," Fogerty said. "I can't quite see a man murdering another man and then reporting it to the nearest authority. I'm going to honor your writ of *habeas corpus* on the plea of insufficient evidence, Nicholet."

"Insufficient evidence!" stormed Garland. "I've seen a man hung on less . . . !"

The crack of Fogerty's gavel was like a gunshot in the room, cutting Garland off. "If you don't have more respect for the court, Mister Garland, I'll find you in contempt. It so happens that Nicholet has presented me with three separate occasions within the two days prior to his death that Carter John had fights with three other men. Why didn't you swear out warrants for them, too, Mister Garland?"

"Because they weren't guilty," Garland raged. "My nephew was always having fights. It didn't mean anything."

"That's exactly my point, Mister Garland." Fogerty's smile was icy. "If you've got a release, Nicholet, I'll sign it."

Nicholet stepped forward with the form, and Fogerty signed it. Before Nicholet could pick it up, Lucas was at the desk with more manila-backed legal foolscap, slapping it on the desk.

"Then I wish to put before the court a warrant for the arrest of Paul Hagar on the charge of resisting arrest by force of arms at the old Beaumont ranch. And this warrant for his accomplice, Miss Cheryl Bannister. And subpoenas for Russian Poker, Patrick Drumgriffin, and Jack Willows as witnesses."

The expression that filled Fogerty's face chilled Hagar. All the wry triumph left it. The eyes turned to ice, swinging toward Hagar.

"How do you plead to this second charge?"

"He can't plead anything but guilty," said Lucas dryly. "And the old Beaumont place is not in the disputed territory. Therefore, the action comes directly under the jurisdiction of county authority."

"If you will look under the release you have just signed, Judge Fogerty, and the writ of *habeas corpus*," said Nicholet, "you will find another writ, which I now take the opportunity of presenting for the court's consideration. It is a plea of *autre fois acquit*. Whether the defendant was guilty of resisting arrest or not, the alleged resistance was contiguous to, and a part of, the first charge of murder . . . seeing that the arrest was being made upon a warrant issued for that primary charge. Therefore, to place him in custody upon the charge of resisting that arrest would be tantamount to placing him in jeopardy a second time on the same charge, which is prohibited by the Constitution of the United States."

"Nicholet!" Lucas had taken a jerky step toward him. "You had it already prepared. You can't. . . ."

"I think you will find precedent for my allegation," smiled Nicholet benignly. "In the case of the Territory of Wyoming versus Harris, two-sixty U.S., three-six-seven, the defendant was acquitted of a murder charge and subsequently prevented from a second arrest on a charge contiguous to the primary accusation by a writ of *autre fois acquit*."

"I remember the case well," said Judge Fogerty. "I sat on it."

"You can't honor such an absurd writ," cracked Lucas, whirling on the judge. "He had it prepared even before he presented the original writ of *habeas corpus* . . . even had it on your desk. Do you call that proper court procedure? How can you sit there and condone such machinations of a shyster like that?"

"Will I have to fine you in contempt, Mister Lucas?" said Fogerty. A smile struggled with Fogerty's cold lips for a moment, then faded. "There's nothing particularly improper about the procedure. Where the writ is . . . or when it was prepared . . . are irrelevant. You yourself had the second warrant prepared before you even knew whether or not I'd honor the first. I've signed the defendant's release. The ruling stands. You have the authority neither to hold Hagar on the murder charge nor to arrest him again. Case dismissed."

Chapter Ten

A small wind was raising flurries of dust and whirling them across the ruts in the streets and dropping them. The silence had left. In its place was a sullen rise and fall of talk all along Center from the temporary courthouse to the last saloon at the other end. Hagar and Nicholet were the first to reach Carey at the bottom of the stairs. They could hear Garland tramping down behind them, berating Lucas.

"*Autre fois acquit!* Who ever heard anything like that? How the hell did you let them slip a fast one by you so easy? By God, you and Steele are both alike . . . sawdust for brains and dishwater for backbones. I'm canceling your retainer right now."

Carey stepped aside as Hagar and Nicholet reached him. "From the sound of things, Hagar's free."

"As a bird." Nicholet smiled.

They moved out onto the boardwalk, with Garland shouldering roughly through the door after them. He was so choked with rage that he could hardly speak.

"This isn't the finish, Hagar," he said. "Not by a long shot. No man can murder my nephew in cold blood and get off."

He wheeled and stepped off the curb, moving stiffly to his 'punchers where they stood in a tight knot with Sheriff Steele.

"I've got to hand it to you, Napoleón," Hagar said. "You had my head swimming with all those legal technicalities. I still don't know why I'm free. You even had that second writ for the judge. That was the smoothest job of work I've seen in a long time."

Nicholet's grin was pleased and embarrassed at the same time. "I knew it must be obvious to them that their original charge wasn't too strong, and figured Lucas would have something else up his sleeve in case Garland couldn't get you before you reached the judge. That charge of resisting arrest was only one of a dozen charges I arranged to circumvent." He put his hand on Hagar's shoulder. "Perhaps you realize it's better to accept the friendship of those who offer it here than to try to stand alone."

Hagar studied his mild, little face, his friendly smile. "Perhaps I do," he said.

"Let's go," Carey said. "I'll give you your gun back at the edge of town."

Hagar turned to him. "You can give it to me now. I'm free."

"You're leaving, Hagar. Garland isn't through yet, and I'm not having any shoot-out in my town."

"Hold on. You don't have the authority to do this."

Carey patted his shotgun. "This is my authority. I'm hired to keep peace in this town. If I have to kick a man out to do it, I will. Now march."

Nicholet caught Carey's arm. "Now, Chip. Take it easy. Hagar will be safer here in town than he would be outside. At least, you can keep an eye on him. If Garland gets him alone. . . ."

"I can't spend all my time protecting a fool who didn't know dynamite when they put it in his hand," Carey said. "I've gone a long way for you already, Nicholet. But I'm not having any more trouble in my town, and that's final. I said march, Hagar."

Glancing down at the shotgun, held in that competent

hand, Hagar shrugged helplessly and started moving down the street. Garland and his men had begun moving, too. Jack Willows cut across the street alone and pushed through the batwings of the Poker Pot. The other 'punchers were spreading out along the street. Garland and Steele began walking toward the south end of town, twenty feet ahead of Hagar and Carey.

"See what I mean?" the marshal said. "They're stirring up something already. Drumgriffin's in the Poker Pot. Now keep moving."

Jack Willows came back out of the Poker Pot and stopped at the curb, staring across the street with a thin smile, his weathered cheek bulged by the inevitable chew. Then the outside stairway of a building ahead began to tremble. Hagar looked up to the windows and saw the sign: **N. Nicholet, Attorney at Law**. Then Cheryl Bannister issued from the door of the covered stairway. She stopped momentarily, staring at Hagar. The Basque coat of black velvet was tailored snugly at the waist, emphasizing the swell of her breasts; sunlight glittered transiently on the jet passementerie trimming her skirt. Then she broke toward Hagar.

"Paul, you're free!"

"Cheryl," he said sharply. "I was wondering where you were."

He stopped as she reached him, catching his elbows, a shining relief in her eyes. "Since I was an accomplice in your escape, Nicholet thought it would be better for me to stay under cover until he obtained your release. Oh, Paul. . . ."

"Oh, Paul . . . is it?" Drumgriffin said.

Cheryl's lips were still parted. Slowly she turned to stare across the street. The Irishman had come out of the Poker

Pot and was standing beside Jack Willows. In the shadow of the overhang, the expression on his face was not clear. But his eyes glittered like naked steel.

Garland was standing before the hitching rack in front of the building housing Nicholet's office, and he called across to Drumgriffin. "What did I tell you, Pat? She didn't help Hagar escape just because she liked the way he parted his hair. Are you going to let him do that? Are you going to let him cut you out?"

"Shut up, Garland," Carey called. "Don't goad him. Can't you see he's drunk?"

"Drunk, am I?" Drumgriffin's voice was ugly. He stepped off the curb, ducked beneath a hitching rack, and started across the street. He may have been drinking, but his movements were as lithe, as smooth, as a cat's. He was staring fixedly at Hagar, and the muscles along his jaw were knotted with rage.

Carey jabbed Hagar with the shotgun. "Move along, damn you! I told you I wasn't having this in my town." The tip of his gun was so painful, biting into Hagar's side, that he could not help lurching forward. Carey kept crowding him, muttering in a savage voice: "Damn them. Needling him like that. Willows was filling him full of it in the Poker Pot. I'll bet my bottom dollar they've been goading him to this ever since Cheryl got you away. Break it up, there, let Hagar through."

With Cheryl hanging on his elbow, Hagar had come up against a knot of men packed closely across the boardwalk. He saw half a dozen E Bar G 'punchers behind the crowd, pushing and elbowing, keeping the press tight.

"I can just hear them down in Laramie now," Garland called mockingly. "From the tracks up to Fifteenth Street. In every saloon along Gambler's Row. How a drifter stopped in and took Drumgriffin's woman. Whipped him first, up at the Bloody Quarter, and then took his woman."

Drumgriffin began running, his voice strangled with rage. "Nobody'll say that. Not about Drumgriffin. Nobody whipped me. Damn you, Hagar, you aren't getting her! She's mine, and. . . ."

"Drumgriffin!" Carey's flat voice was like a slap against the Irishman's roaring tone. "Hagar's unarmed. If you pull that gun, I'll cut you in two."

Drumgriffin slowed, showing the befuddlement of drink in his puzzled frown. In his rage, he had started to pull his gun, and it was halfway out of the holster. Carey swung toward him, the shotgun covering his belly. The marshal backed into the crowd, jabbing viciously with the butt of his Greener while he kept its muzzles covering Drumgriffin.

"Break it up, damn you, let us through!"

But the 'punchers were pushing the townsmen back every time they tried to spread out, and then Garland shouted. "He wouldn't shoot an *unarmed* man, Pat. Not even Carey could get away with murder."

Still coming forward in that faltering, undecided way, Drumgriffin let go his gun and slapped his hands to his gun belt, unbuckling it with a vicious tug. The heavy cartridge belt and holster slid off his hips and onto the ground. Carey saw he couldn't force a way through the crowd. He caught Hagar's elbow with his free hand, wheeling him down off the curb, trying to get him around the crowd before Drumgriffin reached them. There was surprising strength in the marshal's hand, and the first tug took Hagar off balance. Drumgriffin broke into a lunging run across the last few feet, shouting at Hagar.

"You're yellow . . . you're running away."

Hagar wheeled back.

"No, you don't!" Carey shouted.

He tried to spin Hagar around once more with that hold on his elbow. But somebody shouted in the crowd, and a sudden surge from behind spilled the townsmen down off the curb into Hagar and Carey. Hagar saw an E Bar G 'puncher heave into Nicholet, knocking him down. Carey had to let go of Hagar and spin around to keep from being pitched off his feet by the rush of men. At the same time, Drumgriffin crashed into Hagar, knocking him back against the crowd.

Hagar saw the man's black brows twisted above him, the man's great fist smashing down at him. With pain shattering all his senses, it was only animal reaction that made him drop to his knees beneath the man's next blow. He heard the Irishman's gust of air as the man missed and felt Drumgriffin come up against him. He threw himself blindly off his knees into the man.

Drumgriffin was taken off balance, and he staggered backward. Hagar regained his feet, following the man in a rush. Drumgriffin tried to recover. Hagar's blow caught him in the belly. The man gasped, came in against him, grappled him. And for the first time, straining against Drumgriffin in the hot dust of the street, Hagar felt fully the awesome strength of the man.

Hagar was a big man himself, broad through the shoulders. But his frame was more rangy, not packed so densely with the thick musculature that writhed across Drumgriffin's immense torso. Drumgriffin shifted his weight suddenly, tearing one arm back. But Hagar blocked the blow, grappled the arm. Again they were locked together.

"All right," Carey was shouting behind them. "Line up against those walls. If this has to be, it has to be. But if one of you makes a move, I'll cut you down. I swear I mean it this time!"

Then Drumgriffin shifted again, gave a prodigious heave. Hagar tried to throw his weight against the lunge. But the force of those great, knotting muscles checked him, and the Irishman's great weight carried him off his feet. He hit the ground so hard he was stunned. Drumgriffin's body crashed on top of him, emptying his breath out in a sick gust. He heard the man grunt, and a fist smashed into his face. The pain of it blinded him.

Dimly he felt Drumgriffin shift, heard the man grunt again. With the last vestiges of his will, he threw an arm up. He felt the stunning impact of the Irishman's fist across his elbow and knew he had blocked the blow from a more dangerous spot. Drumgriffin tried to sweep the elbow aside and strike again. Hagar rolled the other way, bringing his other elbow up into the Irishman's face. He heard the sharp crack of bone, the man's gasp.

With a tigerish fury, Hagar fought from beneath the man. Just before he was free, Drumgriffin lashed out a boot. Hagar was already rolling to his feet, but it caught him in the belly. It knocked him backward, sickened by the kick. He tried to gain his feet. But the man came into him before he was set, shouting some wild Gaelic oath.

"Arragh!" he roared, and Hagar's head rocked to a blow. *"Arragh!"* he bellowed, and Hagar took a second blow in the body.

Hagar tripped on something and fell. Planks clattered beneath him, and he realized he was on the boardwalk. They had fought out of the street. He tried to roll over and come up against the wall of the Poker Pot. But Drumgriffin had jumped after him. He caught Hagar, as Hagar came up, and hit him again and knocked Hagar through the window.

There was a great smash of glass. Hagar fell to the floor on the inside, part of the window frame still clinging to him.

He rolled over in the shards of broken glass, seeing Drumgriffin jump right through the window after him.

He rolled over again, coming to his hands and knees. But he saw that he could never gain his feet before Drumgriffin reached him, and he threw himself at the man in a tackling dive. It drove the Irishman backward. He struck the wall with a stunning crash. Pinned against the man, Hagar tried to break and straighten up. But Drumgriffin caught him with both hands before he could pull away, spun him around, and hit him.

Hagar staggered backward into the batwings. They popped open, and he pitched through. He hit the boardwalk on his back, flopped helplessly over, rolled off the curb. He heard the batwings squawk again as Drumgriffin charged out. Groggily he came to his hands and knees, trying to rise in time to meet the man's rush. It seemed a painful effort to move. He had only a hazy impression of Drumgriffin crashing into him. He threw up one arm to block a blow.

It smashed his guard aside and knocked him backward. He would have fallen, if he hadn't staggered against the four-by-four support of the wooden overhang. Sagging there, he had the dimmest impression of Drumgriffin coming in again, breathing gustily, of the crowd behind the man, of Little Al's voice coming from somewhere.

"What'd I tell you? Ain't no man in the world can lick Drumgriffin. Hagar never licked him that first time. Nicholet was lying."

"Oh, stop him, Napoleón, he'll kill Paul!"

That was Cheryl's voice, cutting through Little Al's. It did something to Hagar. His head had been spinning, his will had been dissipated by the pain in him. But the sound of her voice crystallized something in him.

He straightened in time to catch Drumgriffin's rush. The

Irishman's sweating body smashed Hagar back against the support. But Hagar blocked the first blow. And in that next instant, knowing this was his last chance, knowing he would not have the strength to rise, if Drumgriffin got him down again, he gathered himself. As Drumgriffin shifted violently to strike, Hagar crossed his arms in front of his face and let them both go. All the power of his big shoulders exploded behind them. They knocked Drumgriffin's blow aside. Drumgriffin's face was directly in front of Hagar, when his elbows struck it, first one, then the other.

The Irishman was knocked away. Giving him no time to recover, Hagar lunged after him. Bloody, panting, shirt ripped half off, Hagar struck for the man's belly. The Irishman doubled forward with a sick gasp. Hagar hit him in the face. Drumgriffin straightened up, shock turning his face blank. Staggering back, the Irishman tripped in a wheel rut.

Before he could go down, Hagar caught him again and hit him in the belly. Again Drumgriffin doubled over. Again Hagar hit him in the face. Again he was straightened up.

The man made a dazed attempt to shift, to dodge the next blow. But Hagar kept in close, driving the man back, bitterly, desperately, knowing this was the last time, knowing he had to finish it now or be finished himself.

Each blow was like tearing his heart out. His arms were like lead. He sobbed with every step. Half the time he was holding Drumgriffin on his feet with the blows. It got so all he could feel was the shock of his own fists against the man. It got so all he could see was that great body in front of him, jerking with each blow.

He drove Drumgriffin clear back across the street, and finally knocked him into the line of E Bar G horses hitched at the rack in front of Little Al's. The ponies whinnied wildly, kicking at Drumgriffin, rearing and fighting to tear loose. One ripped the reins free and whirled to smash into the milling crowd. Hagar lurched in to punch Drumgriffin again, knocking him back into the slot left by the horse.

The Irishman staggered back into the hitching rack, and was stopped by it. Hagar could see him try to set himself, and knew he couldn't let the man use the rack's support. He threw himself at Drumgriffin with a sodden gasp. His body flipped the man over the rack and curb, with Hagar on top. He got to his knees above Drumgriffin and caught his hair and smashed his head against the curb.

The Irishman stiffened beneath Hagar. Hagar tried to lift that massive head and smash it against the curb again. But he did not have the strength. He sagged against Drumgriffin, sobbing with exhaustion. Then he realized the man was limp beneath him. He pulled himself to his knees, staring with glassy eyes at the beaten, bloody body beneath him. He swayed there, hearing the crowd gathering. There was an awed, whispering sound to their movements, their voices. At last Drumgriffin made a moaning noise, and his head moved slightly. Hagar could not recognize his own voice. It was a strangled croak.

"You finished?"

Drumgriffin tried to open his eyes, tried to speak. Only a guttural noise came out. Then Hagar felt a hand on his elbow, heard a voice in his ear, gentle, compassionate, final.

"Yes, Paul. He's finished. It's all over now."

Chapter Eleven

It was the same room, in the Pioneer House, with its iron bedstead, its cracked, china washbowl. Hagar peeled off his torn, bloody shirt, and dropped it on the chair, staring dully at himself in the clouded mirror. His right eye was blackened, swollen almost shut. The whole left side of his face was puffed up and laced with open cuts. Great, purplish bruises mottled his ribs.

Cheryl had brought him here, and then had gone back downstairs for hot water and towels, and, when he heard the door open behind him, he thought it was she.

"I thought I'd seen some fights in my days," Missouri Carnes said. "They were just tea parties."

Hagar wheeled, then winced. The stooped man was standing in the doorway, a wry grin on his horse face. Hagar tried to answer it, and winced again at the pain any movement of his mouth caused him. He took a stiff pace to the bed and sat down on it.

"I'm beat, Missouri. I'm dead-beat."

"You oughta see the Irishman," Missouri said. He shambled on into the room. "I just hit town, when it started. I'm glad I didn't miss it."

A wave of nausea swept Hagar, and he leaned against the rusty head of the bed, closing his eyes. "What happened to you the other night?"

Missouri said: "I waited till I was sure you were all right, then I took out after the bushwhacker. He led me a merry chase before I lost him. Time I got back, the posse was milling around Cotton Creek, and I thought I'd better clear out. I still think I can get more done if nobody knows our connection."

"Drumgriffin came down to have a look at the wagon," Hagar said. "I followed him back to that old Beaumont spread. He met Cheryl there. Claimed he didn't shoot at me."

"He was telling the truth. The man I followed headed north. I never got close enough to find out who he was."

"Poker thought it was a fourth party," Hagar said.

Missouri pulled out one of his inevitable stogies. "You mean somebody besides Garland and the Syndicate and the ranchers?" He bit off the end of the cigar and spat it into the wastebasket. "Could be, Paul. I've run into a couple of things that don't tie in with those three groups."

Hagar was staring dully at the worn rug. "That makes it uglier than ever."

Missouri lit his cigar, nodding. "It does that. You'd better decide what you're going to do quick, Paul. I've been scouting around the Bloody Quarter. Somebody's moving cattle into the hills just below that pass. I saw a Rafter T and a Little Hashknife. That means Muley Banning and Bob Cherington. They're the two strongest ranchers of the War Bonnet bunch. Water's drying up in the flats already. They might be planning to push through the pass to high graze and see what happens."

"Nothing will happen, as far as I'm concerned."

"I don't think they're worried about you. I think they would have gone through already, if. . . ." Missouri broke off as the door was opened again.

Cheryl entered, carrying a big basin of steaming water. She had put on an apron over her dress, her sleeves were rolled above the elbow, steam from the water had heated her bare arms till they were flushed pink. She nodded at Missouri, showing no surprise, backing against the door to close it. Then she walked over and set the basin down.

"Men," she said disgustedly. "The dining room is jammed with them. Potbellied fools who never had a fight in their lives. Waving their arms and yelling and telling each other how it happened like they went through it all themselves. It makes me sick. Missouri, light the lamp so I can see what I'm doing."

Missouri shambled to the vesta lamp on the ivory-topped table, lighting it with his cigar. The smell of camphor filled the room. Light blossomed against the dusk and sparkled against the flash of Cheryl's eyes, half angry, half compassionate. She took the towels and a clean shirt off her shoulder, along with some other things, and put them on the table. Then she wet one end of a towel and began washing the blood and dirt off Hagar.

"It seems I've done this a million times," she said. "You'll never grow up, will you, Paul?"

"Now, Cheryl," Missouri grinned. "He couldn't have got out of this. They were pushing him into it from every side. Garland had failed to get Hagar the other way. It was only a matter of time before Garland got Drumgriffin to try to smash Paul, for one reason or another. Whipping Drumgriffin knocked a big hole in Garland's prestige up here. The Irishman was sort of a symbol of Garland's strength. I think you'll be surprised how this changes things."

Hagar winced as Cheryl began swabbing his cuts with cotton dampened from a small bottle. "What's that?" he asked. "Stings like the devil."

"Carbolic," she told him. "Hold still."

Missouri moved to the window, frowning at the street below. "That's Nicholet coming across. Would he be heading up here?"

"Probably," Cheryl said.

"I'd better duck out, then."

"Finish what you were talking about . . . before you go," Hagar said. "You hinted that something was keeping those ranchers from driving through."

"Men," Missouri said. "On your land."

"Whose men?"

"I don't know. I saw them moving through the timber. It wasn't any of the ranchers' hands. It looked like something funny was up. I'd suggest you ride up tonight and take a look."

"Paul isn't going anywhere tonight," Cheryl said. "He couldn't even sit a saddle."

"I'll be all right. Let me get cleaned up . . . maybe a meal under my belt. I'll meet you on the War Bonnet road in an hour."

"Oh, Paul!" Cheryl said angrily.

Missouri grinned and shambled out. Hagar settled back, looking at Cheryl as she worked. Her nearness was a soothing thing of cool fingers and satiny hands and rich maturity. The scent of her seemed to pervade the room, wholesome, womanly. He watched the golden play of light through her hair, the ripe swell of hip outlined by the dress whenever a turning motion drew it taut. But finally he realized how long it had been since she had looked at him, how she kept her head turned down as she worked.

"Cheryl. . . ."

"There." She cut him off, rising. "It's done. I've brought you a clean shirt. It may not fit."

"That's all right," he said softly. He got to his feet, studying her face.

She was meeting his eyes at last. Her lips were pressed to a thin line. Her eyes were wide, shining.

He saw how close the tears were to the surface.

Then she broke. "Oh, Paul!" She came to him in a rush, the ripeness of her body pressed to his. "I was so afraid. When I saw him hit you like that. . . ." It was a passionate moment. Her body strained against his. Her lips kissed his brow, his cheek, his neck. "I'd have given anything to stop it. He hurt you so much. I couldn't stand it. It was like stabbing me with a knife every time he hit you."

He stopped the frantic movement of her lips by taking her face in his hands and holding it and kissing her on the mouth. With their lips joined, he slid his hands down and encircled her with his arms. Her body was arched like a bow against him. The kiss lasted a longer time than he could measure.

Then, abruptly, she pulled away. She stared up into his face with a strange, savage expression in her eyes. Then she wheeled and walked swiftly to the window. Her hands were locked, and her profile had a set tension.

He followed her, stopping behind her with the scent of her hair in his nostrils. "Don't tell me Drumgriffin is still between us," he said. "You can't tell me you love him, after kissing me like that."

Her voice was bitter. "Do you think you can change a woman's heart simply by whipping a man in the street?"

"I thought you were more of a realist than that. To show a man passion like that and then claim you don't love him."

She slid from between him and the wall, as if wanting to escape physical contact, turning stiffly. "That was animal," she said. "That kiss. I never denied you attracted me that way. Love is something more."

He caught her arm. "How much more?"

But she would not meet his eyes. She tore free, turning to pace across the room, hands still locked together. "Do we have to go through this again?"

He smiled ironically, despite his anger. "This is just like

Denver all over again, isn't it? Can't we ever get together without fighting, Cheryl?"

"We could, if. . . ." She broke off as a knock sounded on the door. Her eyes flashed in anger, then she turned toward the door. "Napoléon? Come in."

The door was opened, and the little lawyer stepped through. The hall outside was dark, and the light caused him to blink his pale eyes. He looked from Cheryl to Hagar, smiling apologetically. "I didn't mean to interrupt anything."

"It's all right," Hagar said.

"I thought perhaps you'd be ready to consummate the deal."

"You've got the cash?"

"We'll have to wait till the bank opens tomorrow," Nicholet said. "But if you bring the deed to my office, we can dispose of the necessary paper work. We can leave the deed in my safe, and I can give you a receipt. The sooner everybody knows that quarter section is out of your hands, Hagar, the safer you'll be. Garland's still in town, and Poker's been busy collecting his saloon toughs all afternoon. They both know this thing can't go on much longer, and they're both going to make another bid."

Cheryl frowned at Hagar. "Does this mean you're selling to the small ranchers?"

He looked sharply at her. "That's what you wanted, isn't it?"

An angry flush tinted her cheeks. She started to speak, then clamped her lips shut, and wheeled to stare out the window.

Hagar turned helplessly to Nicholet. "There was a time when I thought I understood women."

Nicholet smiled knowingly. "Don't you know what she really wants?"

"Never mind, Napoleón," Cheryl muttered sharply. She turned, her face tight and set, and picked up the shirt she had brought to reveal a big envelope beneath. "This letter was addressed to you, Paul. It's been downstairs a couple of days. I brought it up."

Nicholet glanced quizzically at the envelope. "A War Bonnet postmark. You have more friends here than I thought."

Cheryl walked stiffly past Hagar to the door, opening it, pausing. "If you still insist on riding tonight, I'll have the cook fix you something to eat."

He took a step after her, holding out his hand. "Cheryl. . . ."

Without looking at him, she went out, closing the door behind her. Hagar let his hand drop, glanced self-consciously at Nicholet, then turned to pick up the shirt from the table.

"What does she really want, Nicholet? You asked me as if you knew."

"Isn't it obvious, Hagar? She doesn't want you to sell the Quarter to anyone. She wants you to keep it."

"But that wouldn't be what she claims she wants. That wouldn't be settling down. It would mean a constant battle to hang onto the Quarter."

"In her eyes, the battle would be finished sometime. And if you won, you would have something worth settling down to. You would have proved you could plant your feet some-where and stick."

"And while they were planted, I'd be the target for every gun in Converse County." Hagar slipped morosely into the shirt. It was tight across his shoulders, but fit fairly well oth-erwise. "Why are women so blind, Nicholet? She was the same way with Drumgriffin. All she knew was that she wanted him to quit Garland right now. She didn't care what it would cost, what it would mean in the end. She blinded herself to everything but the fact that she wanted Drumgriffin out from under Garland."

"Perhaps women see more than we do," Nicholet said. "Perhaps she saw the cost, and still thought it was the only way. Perhaps she knew that unless Drumgriffin had the strength to cut it clean now, he would never have the strength to break free."

Hagar stared at the man. His words seemed to touch something in him. He could not quite define it. He shook his head. "I'm riding to the Quarter, Nicholet. I got word something funny's going on out there."

"If you sign over that deed, you won't have to worry about what goes on out there."

"I'll sign in the morning, when you have the cash."

"You still don't trust me, do you?"

Hagar glanced sharply at the man, then went over and gripped his shoulder, grinning at him. "You saved my life more than once today, Nicholet. I realize that, and I'm grateful. I do trust you. But as long as you haven't got the money, give me a few hours."

"Perhaps what I said about Cheryl has struck deeper than you'd care to admit," the lawyer said.

Hagar frowned intensely. "There are so many things, Nicholet. It's like I'm groping through a fog. When I stepped into it, my way was clear. Now it's not. I want to ride. I want to think."

Nicholet nodded, and moved slowly to the door. Opening it, he turned back, looking at the envelope on the table. "Anybody's liable to pick that thing up, lying around in the hotel mail slot downstairs. I'd mail it to myself care of General Delivery next time."

Chapter Twelve

The War Bonnet road traced a winding way through the black-timbered shoulders of the Laramies. The poplars, the cotton-woods, the aspens sifted the moonlight through their spring foliage to drop it in a dappled filigree across the rutted wagon trace. From somewhere deep in the timber a saw-whet owl kept filling the night with its rasping call. Hagar had ridden a mile from town, when he heard a horse nicker ahead. He pulled off into the jet shadows and held his hammerheaded mare quiet. In a moment another horseman made a soft clatter coming down through the buckbrush from the ridge.

"It's only me, Paul," Missouri said. Hagar pulled out on the road again, and the other man joined him, sitting a nervous little bay. "You sure are careless for a man in your position," he said. "Riding right down the middle."

Hagar smiled wryly at him. "Do you really think so?"

Missouri's cold stogie tilted skyward in his mouth as he grinned. "I guess not. If I know you, you had every man in War Bonnet pinned down before you left."

"I checked enough. Nobody's on my back trail."

"You still came down that road poky as an old mule. Man travels like that, he's either tired or thinkin'. Did you clear anything up?"

Hagar shook his head. "I don't know. Maybe it will be cleared up for me tomorrow. Nicholet says the ranchers will close on my terms."

Missouri removed his cigar to emit a low whistle. Then he looked closely at Hagar. "Then why bother coming tonight? If you're selling tomorrow, why should you care what's going on at the Quarter?"

"I don't want to do anything in the dark, if I can help it. This may be that fourth party. Wouldn't it be better to know who he is?"

"In a way, it would." Missouri bent toward Hagar again. "You sure that's the only reason you came?"

Hagar glanced at him, then lifted his reins. "Let's ride."

It was a ride of black shadows and startling moonlight, of night sounds, of booming wind in the treetops. For five miles south, War Bonnet Valley was no more than a chasm held in the jaws of the mountains. Then the mountains broke, receded, leaving a broad flat that ran for miles in every direction. Here the Texas Trail cut away from the War Bonnet Road, and the two men took it, heading westward toward mountains that were now only shadowy billows in the distant night. The grass was already drying in the more exposed meadows, brown and curly from the sun, and the water in creek crossings was meager and brackish.

"Not much time left," Missouri said. "Summer's going to be pushing all the ranchers in a few weeks. They'll have to get through to higher graze or have a die-up."

Hagar did not answer, lost in thought. Sensing his mood, Missouri began to reminisce, in that ribald way of his, and for a while the old times came alive again for Hagar and filled him with warmth. Then they met the mountains again and began to climb. They passed the cutoff that led to the Cotton Creek ford, where they had been ambushed in the wagon. Ridge toes began to force the trail into looping turns, and they left the trail and climbed one to the hogback that eventually built up into the south wall of the pass. They could see fires winking in the flats below now, where Cherington and Banning were holding their cattle. They began meeting heavy timber, and finally Missouri pulled up.

"We'd better leave our horses here."

They hitched their animals, and moved cautiously through scaly junipers. Bitterroot spattered the ground with pink stars, and the scent of wild roses was a perfume in the air. The peace of it was in strange contrast to the two crouched figures, moving along the ridge. Finally Missouri stopped, pointing downslope. Hagar studied the dark shoulder for a long time before he saw the faint motion of the grass among the rocks of an open park. He looked at Missouri. The railroad man dipped his narrow head, and they began to work down the mountain in tacit understanding.

They found a ravine choked with fir and spruce and buckbrush. They moved down through this, with limber pine standing in ragged silhouette on the bank above them. The ravine finally broadened out into the park. Moss-grown boulders, big as men, studded the open meadow. Crouching behind one, they heard the fretting snort of a horse straight ahead. Hagar took out his Remington and waved Missouri aside.

"Like with that Frenchman at Durango?" grinned Missouri.

"Like with that Frenchman," Hagar told him.

Missouri moved off toward the left, through the boulders. Hagar waited till he was out of sight, then began to work his way down the park in a straight line. He was halfway across, bellied down behind a rock, when the horse stamped. It was so close he jumped. Then, from fifty feet beyond, he heard a loud crackle of brush.

He knew that was Missouri, and rose from behind the boulder. The horse was tethered on the other side, with the man standing by its head, turned in a startled way toward the rattle of brush from downslope. Hagar went right up the rock and off of it onto him.

The horse reared up, snapping its reins free. The man wheeled, trying to lift his gun up to Hagar. But Hagar crashed into him from above with the barrel of his Remington swiping across the side of the man's head. He grunted. His head jerked to the blow. He fell backward with Hagar riding him down.

Hagar went to his knees astraddle him on the ground. The man made a feeble attempt to roll over, more in stunned reaction than in defense. Hagar doubled his shirt front up in a fist, growling at him. "Stay put unless you want another swipe on the head."

The man straightened out, staring up at him with dazed eyes. The frightened horse was still running downslope, its passage making a distant crashing in the buckbrush.

Missouri worked his way into sight from the rocks below. "Did we do all right, Paul?"

"You timed it perfect. Isn't this the barman that used the shillelagh on me the time you pulled me out of Little Al's?"

Missouri frowned down at the man. He was built like a beer keg, with prodigiously long arms. His head was shaven bald. One of his ears had been sliced completely off, leaving a livid patch of flesh, and his face was a maze of scars from a hundred saloon brawls.

"That's Tanglefoot, all right," Missouri said.

Hagar jammed the man back against the ground disgustedly. "Poker's crowd."

"I thought you were a little optimistic, expecting to find that mythical fourth party this easy," Missouri said.

"What's Poker got you up here for?" Hagar asked. Tanglefoot stared at him sullenly without speaking. Hagar lifted his gun again. "I could whip it out of you."

The barman's mouth twisted over broken teeth. "Poker wants us to keep the ranchers in the flats till we get the Quarter," he said. "If they get through to high graze, they'll be safe for three months."

"And it would be the end of summer before they'd have to respond to pressure," Missouri mused. "How many men you got here?"

"Maybe ten," Tanglefoot said.

Missouri started to speak again, then stopped. He looked at Hagar, then wheeled to stare downslope. At the same time, a man called softly from the fringe of timber.

"Tanglefoot, was that your horse?"

Hagar turned toward the voice. It was an impulsive movement. Too late, he realized the error of it. He felt Tanglefoot surge up beneath him. He tried to turn back and whip the man with his gun. Tanglefoot blocked the descending barrel with a thick forearm and sank his other fist into Hagar's stomach. It knocked Hagar back off him, gasping in pain.

"It's Hagar, Calico," the barman shouted. "Get him!"

Missouri stopped that. His gun struck Tanglefoot's head with a dull crack. The barman dropped soddenly back to the ground. At the same time Calico began firing.

Sickened by the blow to his stomach, Hagar writhed behind a boulder. Missouri had dropped behind another, returning Calico's fire. A slug chipped granite off into his face. He dropped down, grimacing. "That was too close for comfort. I'll circle him. You keep him busy."

Missouri crawled away into the night, toward Calico's right flank. Hagar rose up, waited till a gun flash came from timber, and fired at it. There was silence. The smell of black powder turned the night air greasy.

Hagar took off his hat. He lay flat on his belly, so he could see around one end of the boulder. Then, with his left hand, he shoved the Stetson up on top of the rock. In the moonlight, it made a sharp silhouette. Calico's gun crashed again. The hat was torn from Hagar's hand. He fired at the gun flash twice.

When the crash of his gun was dead, he heard a heavy rattle of buckbrush, receding downslope. It came brokenly, as if the man were stumbling, veering.

Hagar took a chance. He got to his feet and darted to the next boulder. No shot. He ran to the next. Still no shot. That crash of brush was growing dim. He rose from behind the last rock and went at a hard run for the trees fifty feet ahead.

Once in the timber he slowed down, panting, and began working his way after that crashing brush at a cautious trot. He gained on the sound, even at this speed. Ahead, he could see where the timber ended. There seemed to be a narrow strip of meadow that dropped off into the box end of a ravine. Then the man was silhouetted between two junipers ahead, staggering into the open.

In the treacherous illumination, his calico vest was a weird dappling of light and shadow against his heavy torso. He tripped and almost fell, caught himself, and staggered on, veering from one side to another. His breathing filled the air with hoarse gusts. Hagar reached the edge of timber in time to see him at the brow of the ravine. He tried to slide down its steep pitch, but it took his feet from beneath him. He flopped over and slid down to the bottom on his belly. He stopped in a heap at the end of his slide. The dust he had raised hung against the night sky like a milky mist. Then it began to settle about him. He rolled over, groaning softly, and came to his hands and knees. He tried to stand,

and fell back down. Then he began crawling down the ravine. Hagar saw what he had been heading for. His horse was hitched in some buckbrush down there.

Hagar was about to move from the trees, when a sound on his right wheeled him. He saw the tall, stooped shape of Missouri Carnes, running up the line of trees from a hundred yards down. "Paul?" he said.

"Here," Hagar said. "That was Calico. He's hit pretty bad."

"The rest of them are coming. They heard the shots. They must think we're the ranchers or something."

Hagar could hear the rattling crash of talus and brush beneath the passage of many horses now. "Sounds like they're coming up this ravine."

"It's the only way to these meadows. The rest is a bluff that runs out of sight. Let's fade. We can't handle a bunch that big."

"I think we can. You stay here at the head. I'll go down to the mouth. They can't get up this box end on their horses. When they reach you, open fire like you were about a dozen men. If it drives them back to me, I'll stop them."

"Paul, you get crazier all the time."

"Damn it, Missouri, nobody's going to use my land for their private battleground. Poker might as well learn that right now. If you don't want in on it, I'll do it alone."

Missouri's smile made his teeth flash whitely in the dark. "Now, this *is* like the old days."

Flinging him a reckless grin, Hagar wheeled and ran parallel to the ravine. There was a scrubby juniper and some warped oak on its brow that screened him as long as he kept low. Before he reached its mouth, where it opened out into the flats of the pass, he saw the first horse plunge around a sharp turn and scramble up toward the box end. Another followed, and another. The labor of their breathing filled the night.

Hagar stopped at the turn, crouched down in a thick growth of thimbleberry. This would be the best place to take his stand. The walls pinched together, forming a bottleneck only a few feet across, through which no more than two horses could go at a time.

When the last of the riders had plunged through, the billowing dust almost obscured them. Hagar could see clear to the box end of the cañon. Calico had reached his horse and was pulling himself up by the stirrup leather, yelling something.

The lead rider came to a sliding halt. "What?" he shouted. There was just enough of a hole in the myriad sounds for that one word to ring out, sharp and clear. And after that, shots.

Missouri made it sound like a dozen men. He must have been fanning. He couldn't hit anything from that distance, but it was enough to scare the hell out of a man. The other riders came to plunging, rearing halts. For a moment it was a wild mêlée down there, with the dust obscuring most of it, the screams of the horses, the hoarse shouts of the men, mingling with the thundering roll of shots.

Then the first few men had their horses wheeled about. Their panic infected the others, and the whole bunch was racing back toward the bottleneck. Hagar saw Calico's horse spin and run after the others. The man tried to hang in the stirrup leather but finally dropped off, rolling out of sight in the dust. Then the first men were nearing the bottleneck, and Hagar opened fire.

The lead horse was already in a frenzy. At the first two shots, it started rearing and plunging. The rider pitched off, and the horse crashed into another, knocking it off its feet.

Both of them rolled to the ground in the bottleneck, kicking and squealing, blocking the opening off from the others.

A man pulled free of the mêlée, whipping his Winchester up, firing at Hagar. With the slug crackling through the thimbleberry, Hagar shot the man out of his saddle.

A trio broke near the rear and ran back up the ravine. Missouri must have had time to reload. He began firing again. They pulled up, their horses spinning and pirouetting wildly. One of them tried to run his animal up the steep slope on one side. Halfway to the top the talus took the horse's feet from under it, and the beast went down.

Emptying his gun at Hagar, a man tried to run his horse right over the two animals, kicking on their backs in the bottleneck. Hagar went flat on his belly, firing. He missed the man and hit the horse. It went down hard and pitched the man over its head. He hit, flopped over, and lay still.

By now the men still ahorse were swinging out of their saddles and seeking cover behind rocks and in the brush on the sides of the ravine. A trio of empty horses was still running frantically back and forth. At last the only sound was the frantic whinnies of those animals. The dead horse lay in the narrow neck, with its rider still sprawled on the ground ten feet beyond. The man Hagar had shot out of the saddle was trying to crawl for cover. He gained a rock and stopped, belly down, as exposed to Hagar as he had ever been.

With the dust settling, the sound dying, Hagar called out: "All right, Poker. It's Paul Hagar. Drop your guns. Gather in the bottom of the ravine. I'll let you walk out of here. You'll keep walking clear back to War Bonnet."

"It's only Hagar," one of the men shouted. "He can't hold us."

"There's a bunch more at the head of the ravine," another man called. "Sounded like a dozen guns."

"That's still not enough to hold us."

"It is when you count us in," a man called from the mouth of the ravine, somewhere beyond the bottleneck. "This is Bob Cherington. Muley Banning and Karatt are with me, and we've got some of our crews. We can see half of you from where we're standing. There isn't cover in there to hide you."

Hagar stared into the inky shadows beyond the bottleneck, trying to make out the cattlemen. But he could see nothing. There was a long silence below, then a general stirring among the men. One of the riderless horses approached the dead animal in the narrow neck of the ravine, sniffing timorously. Then it threw up its head, whinnied, and ran out into the flats.

"You'd better give up, Poker," Hagar said. "You're trapped. You're outnumbered. We can see every move you make."

"Poker isn't here," a man answered.

"Then whoever's there had better come out," Hagar said.

There was another general stirring in the shadows down there. Hagar could see their dark shapes, shifting through the rocks, the bushes. Two of them began to talk in low voices. Finally a man rose and picked his way down to the bottom of the ravine.

"Drop your gun," Hagar said.

The man let the Winchester slip from his hands. One by one the other men came out, dropping their weapons, gathering in an apprehensive, beaten group. There were six of them.

"I'll let you have three horses for the wounded men," Hagar called. "The rest of you walk."

"Hell, that's fifteen miles," one of them complained.

"It'll give you time to think," Hagar said. "Next time Poker sends you out to carry on your own private battles on my land, just remember what happened this time."

They rounded up three horses, brought in Calico and the other man Hagar had shot, and helped them into the saddles. The one who had been pitched into the bottleneck was stirring now, and they put him on the third horse, slumped over the horn. As they began moving down the ravine, there was a rattle of brush, and Missouri crept in beside Hagar.

"So you don't want anybody fighting on your land," he said. Hagar turned sharply toward him, seeing the droll smile on his face. "You take an awful proprietary attitude for a man who's selling out tomorrow, Paul."

"Never mind," Hagar said curtly. "What about Tanglefoot?"

"I don't imagine he'll try to cause any trouble alone. Cherington and Banning will want to see you, won't they?"

"Probably. I'd like to meet them."

"Then I'd better scoot. I'd rather they didn't know our connection yet. Meet you where?"

"Why not at the shack? I'm going back to town, but I have some gear to pack."

Missouri nodded and backed out of the brush. Hagar saw that Poker's men were marching dolefully out into the bottom of the pass now.

"Hagar," Cherington called, "you still there?"

"Yeah."

"How about coming over?"

Hagar slid down the talus slope, starting a small avalanche. Reaching the bottom, he walked through the bottleneck, beating the white dust off his clothes. There were four riders, holding fretting horses in the shadows on the other side of the narrow notch. Poker's men had reached the lowest part of the pass and were turning toward War Bonnet.

"Think that's all for tonight?" Hagar asked.

Cherington spat. "They're through. I never saw one man kick up so much dust. They thought you had an army. We heard the shooting down at camp and came up for a look. Had Poker planted them here to keep us from moving our beef through?"

"He knew you'd be safe, if you reached higher pastures. Whoever got control of the Quarter wouldn't have any lever against you until winter forced you down again."

"You haven't sold to Poker, then?"

"His terms weren't right. Nicholet said you were ready to deal."

"We've been ready a long time. Why don't you come down to camp and we'll talk?"

"My horse is on the ridge."

"Karatt, give Hagar your animal. He can ride up and get his. You can ride double with me back to camp."

A beefy, bowlegged man swung down from a short-coupled horse, handing Hagar the reins. Hagar swung up.

"We'll meet you at camp," Cherington said.

Hagar nodded, wheeling the cow pony to stare after Poker's men. "Why don't you send a man to follow them for a while?"

"I suppose you're right," Cherington said. "With a man like Poker, you never want to take a chance."

Chapter Thirteen

It took Hagar half an hour to get his horse and make his way back down the slope, through the ravine to the pass, and down the pass to the flats. He skirted the fringe of a bedded herd bearing Cherington's Little Hashknife brand, guarded by a circle rider humming an off-key lament about a lost dogie. It was a lonesome sound in the soft night, and it touched something nostalgic in Hagar. Beyond that, he saw Banning's Rafter T brand on the bedded beef, and a Lazy K, which he supposed to be Karatt's. Then the welcome aroma of coffee floated to him and the muted talk of 'punchers around the fire, and he could not deny the warmth it brought. It seemed a long time since he had known the simple friendships of this kind of life.

Two men rose as he rode in past the chuck wagon. He had seen enough of Cherington's tall, commanding figure in the darkness by the ravine to recognize him now. The man's face was squarely framed, with blunt cheekbones and a heavy jaw and shaggy brows so overhanging they almost hid his eyes. His denim jumper and brass-studded Levi's were filmed with dust and almost colorless with wear.

Muley Banning was shorter, his bowed legs, his sloping shoulders, his outthrust jaw giving him all the pugnacity of a bulldog. He stood with rope-scarred thumbs tucked into his sagging cartridge belt, firelight catching a hostile glitter in his sharp, black eyes.

"Took you time enough," he said.

"Slack off, Muley," Cherington told him.

Hagar could see the one called Karatt, squat and thick-set, seated cross-legged at the fire with a plate of beef and beans in his lap. "You can put the horse on the lines," the man said. "I'll strip him later."

Hagar swung down, leading both his animal and Karatt's horse to the rope strung between two scrubby cottonwoods about twenty feet apart. There were already four other animals hitched there. He had finished tying the reins of his two before he recognized the big, whey-bellied, white horse at the far end. He turned slowly, squinting his eyes against the flickering light of the fires until he could see the other figure, standing in darkness beyond. The man chuckled softly.

"I was wondering when you'd notice me, Paul."

"Nicholet came up while we were in the pass," Cherington explained.

Nicholet moved closer to the fire, picking a tin cup out of the wreck pan. "I came up to tell them you were ready to close the deal. I thought it would be welcome news. Coffee, Paul?"

"Thanks," Hagar said. He walked to the fire, holding out his hands. "Still chilly."

"Always is . . . in the evening," Cherington said.

Nicholet handed Hagar a cup of coffee. "You have the papers with you?"

"I told you I'd have them in the morning," Hagar said. "When you get the ten thousand dollars."

"Ten thousand!" It came from Banning like an explosion. He wheeled on Cherington. "I told you they'd work some kind of skin game on us. That mealy-mouthed lawyer and a damn' speculator from the big town." He turned to Nicholet, a pulse pounding visibly in his thick, weathered neck. "This is the last slick trick you pull on us, Nicholet.

130

I've seen you switch saddles so many times in the past month I'm ready to shoot every one of 'em out from under you."

Nicholet held up a pale hand. "Now wait a minute, Muley. . . ."

"Wait, hell!" Banning stooped to pick up a short length of firewood from the pile beside the flames. "If you don't get out of this camp right now, I swear I'll knock you out."

Cherington caught his arm. "Just hold onto yourself a minute, Muley. Maybe Nicholet can explain."

"Yes," Hagar said, looking through the steam from his coffee cup at the lawyer. "Maybe you can."

Nicholet smiled ruefully and held out placating hands. Karatt had stopped eating and sat staring, open-mouthed, at the lawyer. The two cowpunchers at the other fire were on their feet, waiting to back their bosses, and the gimpy-legged cook was limping from the chuck wagon.

"I was hoping it wouldn't come to this," Nicholet admitted. "I was hoping I could close the deal tomorrow morning before Hagar met you."

"I guess you were," Banning said gutturally.

"Let me finish, Muley," Nicholet said. "Hagar wouldn't close for anything less than ten thousand. We couldn't wait any longer, if we meant to get the Quarter. So I offered to meet his price."

"Where the hell did you think you'd get the money?" Banning swore. "We mortgaged our souls to get twenty-five hundred."

"I was going to put up the other seventy-five hundred myself."

Cherington's shaggy brows lifted. "You!"

Nicholet removed his flat-topped hat and ran a handkerchief around the inside of its sweatband. "What is more logical? If Garland gets hold of the Bloody Quarter, I'm the first one he'll smash up here. If Poker gets it, giving his gambling Syndicate control of the town, there won't be any law left in War Bonnet. And how is a lawyer to make a living in a town where there is no law? Either way, I'd be ruined. Isn't it logical that I . . . as well as you . . . should gamble my all in this attempt to gain control for the few decent men in town?"

"Then why did you have to do it under the table like this?" Cherington asked.

Nicholet put his hat back on, looking at Banning's glittering eyes, his rage-filled face. "Because I knew Banning too well. I feared he would do the very thing he is going to do now."

"And you were damned right!" Banning said. "Can't you see what this'll do, Cherington? Nicholet's putting up three quarters of the money. How much of the control does that give him? He'll be able to outvote us on every issue. He'll wind us up in one of them complicated contracts with clauses we can't understand. . . ."

"On the contrary," Nicholet said. "It will be a simple loan. The deed to the Bloody Quarter will be in your names. The only place my name will appear is on the promissory note you sign for the seventy-five hundred. There will be no interest on the money, and the time limit will give you a safe margin in which to repay."

"That sounds reasonable enough," Cherington said.

"Too reasonable," Banning said. "Did you ever see this shyster loan money without interest?"

"This is different," Cherington said. "Nicholet is in this fight as deep as we are, and it sounds like he's making a legitimate offer. For once in your life stop being a hot-headed fool."

"Fool!" Banning was shaking with rage. "If Nicholet can pull one deal under the table, he can pull a dozen. This isn't the first time he's pulled a slick one on us. Telling us Hagar'd settle for twenty-five hundred, and then telling Hagar we'll close for ten thousand. How can you trust a man who plays both ends against the middle like that?"

"He had a reason. You're proving it right now."

"He probably had half a dozen reasons. Garland might even have been one of them. How do we know that seventy-five hundred isn't coming from Garland? Nicholet could set up that contract so the Quarter'd go to Garland on some default of ours, and we couldn't even tell the difference."

"You sure were named right," Cherington said. He was almost shouting, too. "Of all the stubborn, knot-headed mules I ever saw, you take the cake. This is our only way out. Nicholet is willing to throw everything he's got into it, willing to give us a chance, and you think. . . ."

"I think maybe somebody else in our crowd made a deal under the table, too," Banning said. "Why are you so quick to defend a swindle like this? It's as crooked as they come."

The blood drained from Cherington's face. "Muley, I've taken as much of your pigheadedness as I can stand. I won't be responsible for what I do, if you go on talking like that."

"I don't think you ever were responsible," Banning said. "I'm not risking my neck for a shyster that tells a different story on every side."

"Then you might as well take your cattle back to the flats and let them die up."

"That's exactly what I'm gonna do," Banning stormed. "It's better'n being trapped in the high grass with a man who'd stick a knife in your back."

Nicholet stepped around the fire, putting a hand on his arm. "Wait a minute, Banning."

"Let go of me, damn you!" Banning snarled, wheeling away. He held the length of stout wood for a moment, as if to strike Nicholet. Then he threw it from him with a disgusted curse, glancing viciously at the other man. "Karatt, you coming?"

"Don't be a fool, Karatt," Cherington said. "You follow this jackass and you'll end up with a bunch of dead cows."

Karatt put his plate and fork down, grunting as he got to his feet. "I don't know, Bob," he said, staring at the fire. "There's a lot in what Muley says. I wouldn't want to go into this blind."

"Damn you all for a bunch of lily-livered lamb lickers!" Cherington said. He wheeled to pace away from the fire, rubbing savagely at the back of his neck. "If you haven't got the guts to take some kind of gamble on a deal like this, you might as well go back where you come from."

Karatt held out his hand. "Now, Bob, you ain't got no right. . . ."

"Get out," Cherington said disgustedly. "I'm sick of coddling the bunch of you. I'm sick of your whining."

A hurt look came into Karatt's heavy-jowled face. He glanced helplessly at Hagar, then turned to follow Banning's bulldog figure to the horse lines.

Banning was already whipping into the saddle of his dun and wheeling it out into the night, calling hoarsely to the circle rider. "Si, start getting them Rafter cattle on their feet and cutting them out. We're dragging."

Cherington quit pacing, quit rubbing at his neck in that exasperated way. He walked listlessly to the fire and sat down on a log, staring into the flames.

Nicholet shook his head sadly. "And there you have a prime example of what wonderful accord the War Bonnet cattlemen always find themselves in."

The fire snapped softly. Cherington took a deep breath. "I guess I shouldn't have got mad." He shook his head. "Muley's just been rubbing me raw. I guess we were all jumpy, waiting here for the push."

"You've still got the most cattle," Nicholet said. "If you push through, maybe the rest will follow."

"Banning won't come now," Cherington said. "When he gets set against something, a twenty-mule team couldn't pull him back. I may have most of the cattle, but he's got most of the cash. With him out of it, you wouldn't get your full ten thousand anyway."

"You understand why I did it that way," Nicholet said.

Cherington nodded. "Muley proved you were right. I'm sorry you didn't swing it before we got together like this."

Nicholet looked at Hagar. "You wouldn't come down to eight thousand?"

Cherington rose, slapping dismally at his batwing chaps. "Wouldn't do much good if he did, Nicholet. Banning will have half the ranchers with him now. The rest of us couldn't hold the Quarter, even if we got it."

"Hagar held it alone," Nicholet said.

Cherington glanced at Hagar. "For a couple of weeks. Do you think he could hold it for a season . . . with somebody waiting to stampede our beef every time we tried to push through that pass?"

Nicholet was silent for a long space, staring into the snapping fire. "I guess there's nothing more I can do, then, is there?" he said at last. He turned indifferently to Hagar. "If you want my company back to War Bonnet, we can go now. It wouldn't be safe for you to ride back alone with that deed on you."

"You're assuming I have it on me," Hagar said.

Nicholet's brows rose. "It could hardly be any place else,

if I judge you right. You're a little more subtle than to mail it to yourself a second time."

"It's safe, Nicholet. If you want to ride now, go ahead. I have to clean up something here."

The man stared at him for a moment, then tipped his hat to them, and walked over to mount his horse.

Hagar watched him ride out into the night. "He didn't seem as sorry as he should be."

Cherington looked after Nicholet. "He hides what he feels. I don't doubt this hit him below the belt. He loses as much as we do."

Hagar realized he still held his coffee. It was cold, and he dumped it back into the pot and moved the pot back on the fire. Then he moved over to Cherington. His weariness had hit him abruptly, leaving him sodden, apathetic. He lowered himself heavily to the log beside Cherington. The cook was clattering softly through the pots and pans at the chuck wagon. A steer was bawling plaintively out of the bed grounds. The coffee began to chuckle.

"Good sounds," Hagar said idly.

"You talk like cattle."

Hagar looked at the old rope scars on his sinewy hands. "I've run beef in my time. Mostly speculation, though. Buying and selling." He watched Cherington move the pot off the flames and pour two cups. A strange thought was in his head now, formed perhaps in these last moments, when he had seen these two men fighting so bitterly over their stakes, or perhaps formed long before that, without his even being aware of it. "How does it feel to own your own piece of land, Cherington?"

Cherington looked at him quizzically. "Do you think men like me and Muley would fight so hard to keep it if it wasn't good, Hagar? You look like a drifter to me. Done this sort of thing all your life. Made a strike . . . cleared out. What have you got when you do that?"

Hagar sipped at his coffee. "Not much. You're right."

"Ten thousand dollars? How long does that last you? A few weeks, a few months. Then you blow it somewhere. Gambling. A woman. A new speculation. And you're right back where you started." Cherington picked up a handful of earth. "A piece of land is always there," he said. "You come home to it every night. That's good . . . coming home. Riding down your fence, through your gate. Lights in the windows. The door opens. Your woman's standing there, waiting. That's what land's like, Hagar. A woman. A good woman. You know she'll always be there."

Hagar felt something close up in his throat. "Funny you should make that comparison," he said.

Chapter Fourteen

After leaving Cherington's camp, Hagar scouted the pass carefully on the way up to the shack, finding no sign of Poker's men. Then he rose to the spiny ridge behind the shack and worked his way down through timber from above. It was the logical cover ambushers would use, but it was empty. A night wind sobbed through the poplars as he approached the forlorn cabin, huddled against the rocky slope. Streaks of light showed through where chinking had fallen from between the logs. Missouri's chestnut stamped complacently at the rickety hitching rack before the door. It sent a feeling of security through Hagar to know the droll, unruffled man was waiting inside for him.

He swung stiffly out of his saddle and made his tie at the rack. The wounds from the fight were beginning to ache and throb now. Weariness seemed to pervade his very bones, filling him with the beginnings of stupor. He fumbled at the latch, pushed the door open, stepped in. Then he stopped.

"If you pull your gun or step back out the door," Poker said, "Little Al will blow Missouri's head off."

Hagar felt sick at his stomach with the shock of it. He still held the door with one hand, staring blankly at the three of them. Poker sat at the table, holding a pack of cards he had been idly shuffling. Missouri was seated on one of the bunks. Nobody but he could have grinned so foolishly, so drolly, under the circumstances. But there was a fine beading of sweat on his bony forehead. Little Al stood at his elbow with the muzzle of a .45 Colt pressed against his temple.

"They caught me with my pants down, Paul," Missouri said. "I'm sorry."

"You made a mistake thinking I wouldn't be with my men," Poker said.

"I didn't think you'd want to dirty your hands on that kind of a job," Hagar said.

"Little Al and I were on this side of the pass, when the shooting started," Poker explained. "We tried to join the men, but you already had them bottled up. When Cherington joined you, we decided the odds were a little too big to go on. We figured you'd be coming back here. Sit down."

Hagar walked slowly to the table and sat down in the remaining chair.

Poker put away the cards. "Missouri saved your life in Little Al's that time," he said. "Now we catch him coming to the shack here, just after you trapped my men. That would indicate he helped you trap them. Nobody but a good friend would have sided with you against such odds. So we assume Missouri is a good friend. We assume you will sacrifice as much for him as he was ready to sacrifice for you."

Hagar stared at Poker, his voice heavy. "And you want the deed."

"We know you received a bulky letter with a War Bonnet postmark just before you left town. We know you had reasons to keep it on you till tomorrow morning."

"Is the mail clerk at the Pioneer House one of your spies, too?"

"It doesn't matter. Put the papers on the table or Little Al will shoot your friend in the head."

Hagar glanced at Missouri. Then, without speaking, he

opened his shirt, unbuckled a specie belt, pulled it out. From this he took the envelope.

"Paul . . . !" Missouri said disgustedly.

"What else could he do?" Poker said. "A cheap price for a friend's life." He took a piece of paper from his pocket, unfolded it, laid it before Hagar. "The papers are no good, of course, without the transfer. This is a quit-claim. We even brought pen and ink. Fill in the date as of June Sixth."

Hagar studied the form. "You haven't filled in the party of the second part."

"That will be taken care of. You just sign as party of the first part."

"Paul," Missouri said. "Don't be a fool. Once you sign that deed, you're a dead duck. They don't mean to let us go. They can't, when we know what we know."

"On the other hand, if he doesn't sign it, we'll kill you now," Poker said. "Quite a dilemma, isn't it?"

"I'll sign . . . on one condition," Hagar said.

"You aren't in any position to pose conditions."

"I think you'll take it. I want you to let Missouri go now. I'll sign, when he's clear."

Poker's face showed no reaction. "If I meet your condition, you'll have to meet mine. Play a game of Russian poker with me, and I'll let Missouri go, no matter which of us wins."

"Boss!" cried Little Al. "Are you crazy? After you got what you want? You did this once before and lost a chance at that deed."

"The deed has nothing to do with this, really," Poker said. The little muscles were tightening up around his mouth. The first shine was coming to his eyes. He leaned toward Hagar. "This is one time you'll have to play, isn't it, Hagar? I've been trying to get you in a game for a long time, and you can't back out now. Maybe you could turn down ten thousand dollars, but you can't turn down Missouri's life."

Hagar stared into the man's fixed eyes. "How do I know you'll keep your word, if I lose?"

"Did you ever know me to go back on it?"

"Did you ever play for such high stakes?"

Poker flipped the deed contemptuously. "Do you call this high stakes? Penny ante, Hagar. It's the biggest thing that ever hit War Bonnet, but it isn't worth a white chip compared to Russian poker."

Little Al bent toward Poker. "Listen, you promised me . . . you promised all of us!"

"I promised you I wouldn't play poker until that deed was in our possession. We've got it now, haven't we? The quit-claim will make it ours."

"But you, boss. . . ."

"Yes, me." Poker's lips peeled off the words in more of a grimace than a smile. "I devoted my life to Russian poker before we got the Bloody Quarter, Al. I'll go on devoting my life to it, after we get it. Can't you see how incidental it is? Right now it's the only lever by which I get another game. It isn't often I can play with a man of Hagar's caliber. They all think he's got guts. Just because he whipped Drumgriffin? Just because he stood up to Garland? We'll see. Sign, Hagar. It's the only way."

"Don't do it, Paul, don't be a fool," Missouri said. He was leaning forward in the bunk, with Little Al's gun pressed so tightly against his head a ridge of white flesh circled the muzzle.

Little Al was staring at Poker, shaking his head, that bucolic helplessness slacking his lips. "I never knew how crazy you really were, Poker. You always said you'd give the world for one round. I guess I never really took it in. You've got it in your hands. You'd be the biggest man in War Bonnet."

"I'm the biggest man in War Bonnet right now," Poker said. His eyes were shining. There was a rapt smile on his face. "That's the way it makes you feel, Al. Big. Like you could move the world." He flipped the gun from beneath his coat, snapped out the cylinder, emptied all but one slug from the chambers, snapped back the cylinder. Then he put the gun down. He straightened in the chair, an exalted look on his face. "Sign, Hagar, and we'll start."

"They'll kill you, Hagar." Missouri's voice was a strained whisper. "You don't think this is square, do you? They've got it rigged."

"It isn't rigged!" The womanish cry whipped from Poker, and he half stood from his chair, face contorted with anger.

Missouri stiffened, too, with the jabbing pressure of Little Al's gun against his head.

Slowly, Poker settled back, trembling visibly.

Hagar stared at him, remembering how before he had tried to reconcile this strange childishness with the gambler's usual impassivity. "I don't think it's rigged, Missouri," Hagar said. "If they wanted me dead, they wouldn't have to go through all this. In fact, Poker, when it comes to your game, I think you're probably the most honest man I've ever met. You may be crazy, but you're the most honest."

A little muscle twitched in Poker's cheek. "Thank you, Hagar," he said solemnly.

None of them spoke then. There was the sputtering of the candle, the hoarse undertone of their breathing, the scratch of the pen. When he was finished, Hagar shoved the quit-claim to Poker. The man barely glanced at it, then shoved it aside.

"Boss," whimpered Little Al.

The cylinder made a sharp, ratcheting sound, turned by Poker's thumb. His eyes had a varnished shine in the candlelight. Staring at Hagar fixedly, he lifted the gun to his temple. He held it there for what seemed an eternity. A faint nausea swept Hagar. Then Poker pulled the trigger.

There was an oily *click*.

In the silence that followed, the three men continued to stare at Poker, as if mesmerized.

Finally Missouri let out a ragged breath. "My God," he said. "He really means it."

For a moment longer, Poker held the gun to his temple. Then the glassy look faded from his eyes, his breath left him in a little sigh. He put the gun on the table. His mouth twitched with a spasmodic grin. "Your turn, Hagar. If you have any ideas about using this shell for other purposes besides the game, remember there are two of us, and only one bullet. And I think Little Al could blow Missouri's head off, even if you did shoot him."

"Paul," Missouri said, "don't do it. Not even for me. I wouldn't do it for you. I swear I wouldn't do it for you."

"I think you would," Hagar said.

He was staring at the gun. He was filled with the same mixture of repulsion and fascination that had come to him before, when Poker had challenged him to the game at Little Al's. But it had not been so strong then.

There was something obscene about it. That bright, glittering gun, lying on the table. Something magnetically obscene that pulled his hand toward it even though every impulse cried out to jerk his hand back.

The cold metal was soothing, somehow, strangely sensuous. He stared at his hand as if it were someone else's, moved by a force outside himself. It lifted the gun. It

143

twirled the cylinder. It pressed the weapon against his head. It tightened a finger against the trigger.

"Paul! Don't!"

Click.

After a while, after a long while, he realized he was pressing the gun against his head so tightly that it hurt. He eased his finger on the trigger. He lowered the weapon to the table.

Missouri's voice was hollow. "God . . . Paul."

Poker picked the gun up, that grimace of a smile on his lips, eyes shining rapturously. "Did you see his face, Al? For a moment I thought he wouldn't go through with it. How sad if he should break so soon! I thought we'd found one of the initiate. Second round."

The rattle of the twirled cylinder. The glitter of nickel plating as the gun was raised. The pause. The pale, stiff grimace, so close to ecstasy.

The *click*.

They began to breathe again. A little ripple of muscle ran through Poker's face. His eyes gained focus, as though he were coming out of a trance. He put the gun on the table. He wiped sweat from his face. He loosened his collar.

"Listen, Paul," Missouri said. "You've done it once. You've shown him you've got the guts. Don't do it again. I'd rather both of us died. I won't let you do it."

"You haven't much to say, my friend," Poker said. "Hagar is a sentimentalist."

Hagar was gazing at the gun again. He wouldn't let it get him this time. He'd just reach out and pick it up and spin the cylinder and pull the trigger.

"Pressure builds up with each one, doesn't it, Hagar?" Poker gave a shaky laugh. "You'll find that. And you'll find it getting you. More and more. At first it's a mixture. Fear

144

and fascination. But fear is the main thing. Then the fascination starts taking hold. If you're one of the initiate, the fascination starts getting you."

Hagar grabbed the gun and twirled the cylinder and pressed it to his head and pulled the trigger.

After the *click,* after the pause, after time stood still, he put the gun back down again. He was trembling. He was sweating.

"It's getting him." Poker was staring at Hagar with avid eyes. "Did you see his face, Little Al? I told you he'd break. Whipping Drumgriffin! What's that compared with this? I told you . . . I told you. . . ."

"Get on with it," Hagar said sharply.

Poker's head jerked a little. Then a shaky laugh escaped him. "Now he's mad," he said. "Now I've made him mad." He picked up the gun. Excitement made his hand tremble. "Of course, Hagar. On with it. You don't really begin to live until the fifth round. And this is only the third."

He spun it. He lifted it. He waited, grimacing triumphantly. Hagar stared fixedly, shocked at the perverted excitement running through him. The *click* made his whole body jerk.

Poker laid the gun down, a strange, lustful huskiness to his voice. "Better than a woman, Hagar. Far better than a woman."

Hagar reached out for the gun. Poker was right. The pressure was building up with each one. And it was more fascination now than fear. The desire to touch the gun was like a strange fire in him. Only the coolness of the metal could quench it. His fingers curved around the butt. He lifted it. He twirled the cylinder. He pressed it against his head.

"Paul, for God's sake . . . !"

Revulsion swept through him. His impulse to fling the gun from him was so strong that his whole arm jerked. Poker threw his head back to laugh, a shrill, insane sound.

"What did I tell you, Al? Did you see that? He's cracking. He licked Drumgriffin, but it doesn't mean a thing. He's cracking."

Click.

The sound stopped Poker's voice. He stared at Hagar, eyes glazed, face shining with sweat. Hagar laid the gun back on the table, watching Poker with steady, bitter eyes. It was amazing how many emotions this could draw from a man. He hated Poker now, with a hatred stronger then any he had ever known before. His voice was brittle with it.

"Go ahead."

Poker laughed again. It was a shaky laugh. He wiped his lips. They had a slack look. He lifted the gun. He twirled the cylinder. He pressed the muzzle against his head.

"Fourth round."

The explosion was deafening. It rocked the room. It wheeled Little Al around till his gun no longer pointed at Missouri. It brought Missouri up out of the bunk.

Hagar found himself on his feet, staring at Poker. The man had pitched over backward. He was sprawled grotesquely on his overturned chair, arms thrown wide, mouth open. Blood was already forming a viscid pool beneath his shattered skull.

"Poker!" It left Little Al, after an interminable time. "Boss!" He sounded like a whimpering puppy. He moved stumblingly, uncertainly to Poker, staring down at the dead man with stunned eyes.

Hagar took a chance and pulled his gun. He didn't need it. Little Al was not even aware of him. The huge man continued to stand above Poker, making those whimpering sounds, shaking his head back and forth as if faced with something completely beyond his belief.

"You got a bottle in this shack?" Missouri said. "I think we all need a drink."

Chapter Fifteen

There was a sick-sweet taste in Hagar's mouth, when he awakened. He lay in the stupor following a deep sleep, orienting himself with difficulty. The bed was softer than his bunk at the shack. Memory began to come. He was in the Pioneer House again. He and Missouri had ridden back to town last night, wanting to report Poker's death as soon as possible. They had gone to Carey first, and he had taken them to Arny Means, the sheriff of Converse County. Means had merely asked them to be around when the coroner's inquest took place.

Hagar pushed the covers off, getting up from bed with great difficulty. The full effects of the fight were reaching him now. He ached in every joint; bruises in a dozen places throbbed unmercifully. He got a razor from his saddlebags. It was a torture to shave. He washed, dressed, went downstairs, and headed straight for the bar. The bar clock showed it to be after noon, and there were half a dozen patrons at the brass rail.

The bartender came down to Hagar, polishing a glass and shaking his head sympathetically. "You look like you need something special."

"Just fill that glass with Joe Barry," Hagar said.

As the man moved down to the fifty-gallon barrel of whiskey in the rack back of the bar, Hagar became aware of the other men along the bar closing in. He half turned, a tension running through his body. But all he saw was a bunch of open mouths and wide eyes.

The man nearest him was pulling a pad and pencil from

beneath his dusty frock coat, clearing his throat. "I'm Harry Myers, *War Bonnet Clarion*, Mister Hagar," he said. "Did you really go fifty rounds of Russian poker to the finish last night?"

Hagar swung back to the bar, putting his elbows heavily on the mahogany. He lowered his face to a hand, rubbed it across his eyes. "Fifty rounds," he said. He shook his head tiredly, making a rueful sound.

"I'd like the story," Myers said busily. "The human-interest end. You know. How it felt. The tension. That madman sitting across the table from you."

"Write it yourself, Harry," Cheryl Bannister said at Hagar's elbow. "Your imagination is good enough. Mister Hagar doesn't want to talk about it."

Myers's mouth opened, and a blank look filled his face. "Yes, Miss Bannister," he said. "Of course. But. . . ."

"Go on now, Harry," she said.

Hagar turned toward her, elbows still on the bar. She wore a dress of watered silk with puffed sleeves and square yoke, an onyx brooch riding the swell of her bosom.

"Thanks, Cheryl," he said in a low voice.

Intense compassion filled her eyes momentarily. She reached out to grasp his arm, her fingers tight. "I know how you must feel. If there's anything I can do . . . ?"

"Just being here is enough," he said.

The bartender slid the glass of whiskey down the bar with a practiced sweep. It stopped precisely before Hagar. He picked it up and downed a long one, eyes squinted against the raw fire of it. Cheryl took her hand from his arm, watching him soberly. Some of the compassion was gone from her face. He sensed a reserve in her manner.

"What is it, Cheryl? Last night, in the hotel room?" he asked.

She looked away quickly, lips compressed.

"I thought it was just a kiss," he said. "I thought it didn't mean that much."

She looked back at him, anger flashing in her eyes. "Finish your drink," she said stiffly. "The inquest's at one. Missouri said he'd meet you here."

He glanced away, trying to find words that would penetrate the wall between them. He shook his head helplessly. "Missouri's up, then?" he said inadequately.

"At ten. He had breakfast with me."

"Think there'll be any trouble?"

"Not with the coroner." Her voice grew thin, almost bitter. "It's Little Al you'll have to watch out for. He brought Poker in this morning about three. They've been holding a wake in the saloon ever since. Little Al swears he's going to get the man who killed Poker."

Hagar lifted his gaze till he could see himself in the bar mirror. Slowly nausea churned up within him. It was more than physical reaction. "That about does it," he said. His voice was guttural and strained. "I don't want to meet Little Al that way. I don't have anything against him. I never thought I'd feel this way about a fight, but it isn't just a fight any more. It's ugly. I'm going to close the deal today. Ten dollars or ten thousand. I don't care who bids first, I'm going to close, and I'm going to get out."

She caught his arm. "I know last night was bad, Paul, but. . . ."

"Don't say it, Cheryl. I won't be jockeyed into something like Drumgriffin. You told me you wanted me to sell out to the ranchers, and, when I said I was going to do that up in the hotel room, you acted like I'd stabbed you in the back. I'm sick of this whole thing, and I'm getting out."

She stared up at him, her underlip quivering, then looked away again, quickly, speaking in a voice too low for the bartender to overhear. "Paul, let's not even talk about it any more. You're still jumpy from last night. You're more upset than you know."

Seeing the hurt he had caused her, he realized she was right. Last night had taken a greater toll than he had realized. In sudden contrition he caught her shoulders, turning her toward him again. "Cheryl, I'm sorry. I guess I am in a mean mood. I feel low enough to eat off the same plate with a snake. Whatever I do, I don't mean to hurt you. You've got to understand that. There's still something between us, and I can't get through it or beyond it, but I don't want to hurt you."

She looked up at him, the anger gone, tears shining in her eyes. "I know, Paul. You'd better go now. Here's Missouri."

She must have seen Missouri in the bar mirror. He came in from the dining room, the droll grin on his horse face. "Looks like you two have been spatting again."

"Never mind, Missouri," Hagar said.

Missouri glanced at Cheryl. Something passed between him and the woman. Then he said: "About time for the inquest, Paul. I'll go with you."

"I won't be here, when you get back," Cheryl said. "I've got shopping to do."

Hagar searched Cheryl's face in that last instant for some hint of what had happened within her, but she would give him none. He passed her, head down, going out at Missouri's side in moody silence.

"What did you do with the papers to the Quarter and that quit-claim?" Missouri asked as they neared the door.

Hagar patted his coat. "Inside pocket."

"You'd better get rid of them, Paul. With your name on that quit-claim, the thing's as good as a signed blank check.

151

Anybody could sign his name on it and own the Quarter."

Hagar frowned. "I wonder why Poker left the party of the second part blank."

"Any number of reasons. Maybe he meant to sell out to Garland."

"Or that fourth party."

"What does it matter? It's like sitting on a keg of dynamite to carry that around. You'd just be a target for all of them again, if they knew you had it on you."

"Where would I put it? Cheryl'd be the target, if I left it in the safe. I wouldn't put her in that position, or you, or anybody. They won't have time to find out I've got it, anyway. All I have to do is hand over the quit-claim to whoever buys."

Missouri sent him a strange glance, then shook his head darkly. "All right, Paul."

As they stepped from the lobby door, a great, brazen blare struck at them. Hagar stared down the street a full block to where a crowd was gathered around Little Al's saloon. A band had formed on the sidewalk, a beefy Teuton puffing at a tuba, a long drink of water pounding a bass drum held on the back of a little boy, a bald man playing a cracked cornet, and a white-haired swamper whanging a triangle. They were all dressed in soiled red coats with stiff, white collars, brass buttons glittering in the sun.

"The local fire department band," Missouri said. "Poker's funeral is going to be the biggest thing that hit War Bonnet since the Christmas flood."

They turned north along the street, away from Little Al's, toward the jail. As they dipped from the shade of the overhang into the bright sunlight, a black hearse rattled by, drawn by a pair of jet mares, followed by a score of curious people, ahorse and afoot, all heading toward Little Al's.

Among the riders Hagar saw Karatt and Banning and half a dozen other dusty cattlemen.

Muley Banning pulled out of the group, when he saw Hagar, bringing his short-coupled dun over to the board-walk. "Did you really do that with Poker?"

"He did," Missouri said.

"Seventy rounds?"

"You trying to make a piker out of him? It was eighty-seven rounds."

"Cut it out, Missouri," Hagar said.

Banning wiped sweat from the grizzled seams of his un-shaven jaw. "By God, I got to hand it to you, Hagar. Maybe we had our differences last night, but I really got to hand it to you. I wouldn't have the guts to do it myself."

"Takes more than guts," Missouri said. "A man has to be a little crazy. You going to the meeting tonight, Banning?"

"What meeting?"

"The ranchers are getting together at Cherington's. He's going to try to persuade them to take Nicholet's offer."

Banning's face darkened. He jerked his reins up. "I sure as hell ain't going. I told him where I stood last night." He wheeled and rode on down the street, a squat, powerful figure in the saddle.

Hagar watched him go, then said to Missouri: "Did staying under cover really help you so much?"

"I have a briefcase full of facts I wouldn't have got, if they knew I worked for the railroad."

"Anything on Banning?"

"You mean why do all Banning's fights with Cherington seem to play right into the hands of Garland or Poker?"

Hagar looked at him, grinning ruefully. "You have got your lines out."

"I haven't been sitting on my hands," Missouri said. He

took out one of his inevitable stogies, studying it. "I know what you're thinking. Poker could have found out from the clerk at Pioneer House that you mailed those Bloody Quarter papers to yourself. But how did Poker know you'd have the papers on you last night?"

"Nicholet told the ranchers I was going to sell to them this morning," Hagar said. "They were the only ones who knew I'd have reason to keep the papers on me last night."

Missouri bit off the end of his stogie. "So the only way Poker could have known was by contact with one of the ranchers."

Hagar stared after Banning again, far down the street now. "Did it ever strike you how similar Carter John's death was to the way we were ambushed at Cotton Creek?"

"You've got to remember Poker didn't know about Carter John's death any quicker than the rest of us," Missouri said. "If Banning had done the job for Poker, wouldn't Poker have known sooner?"

"Maybe Banning didn't do it for Poker."

They were walking north again, and Missouri sent him an oblique glance. "You're thinking of that fourth party again. But Banning's connected with the ranchers."

"He's connected, but maybe he doesn't belong."

"If he was in it for himself, why should he pass the word to Poker that you were carrying the papers last night?"

Hagar shook his head. "I can't add that one."

The offices fronting the jail were full of men—Sheriff Means, a couple of his deputies, Marshal Carey, Judge Fogerty, the coroner. It was an informal inquest, without a jury. They already had a statement from Little Al. The doctor's medical report ascertained beyond doubt that Poker himself had pulled the trigger of the gun that killed him; there were powder burns all over his hand. Finally Missouri gave his testimony, identifying himself with his railroad commission. Then Judge Fogerty simply requested that Hagar sign a statement of his presence at Poker's death and the circumstances involved. As he bent to read it and sign, the noise of the band began to swell. It took him a minute to recognize Chopin's "Funeral March" over the other hubbub.

Carey stepped to the door, pulling angrily at his spade beard. "Looks like they're starting. We're going to be busy with that drunken crowd, or we'd go back with you ourselves. Can you get Hagar into his hotel before they reach it, Missouri? I want him out of sight with Little Al on the streets."

"Can do," Missouri grinned. He hooked a hand in Hagar's elbow, guiding him to the door. The parade was just forming in front of Little Al's with the black hearse pulling away from the boardwalk, the band marching in front. But there were crowds of merrymakers all along the street, issuing from the saloons, gathering in shouting, laughing knots by the hitching racks.

A cowpuncher came reeling through the batwings of the Poker Pot, waving a bottle. "Stop that funeral march! It's time for happy music. Poker's dead, and there ain't a man in War Bonnet that's sorry."

Missouri turned Hagar down toward the hotel.

Hagar asked: "Why did you reveal yourself like that?"

"I didn't want them to pull another Carter John on you."

"They wouldn't. I was clear without your testimony. You didn't even ask them to keep your identity a secret. It'll be all over town before evening. Why did you want everybody to know, Missouri?"

"Now, Paul, it wasn't anything like that."

"I think it was. You made every attempt to keep your connection secret before. It was a big move to reveal yourself. You did it for a reason, Missouri. What was it?"

"There he is," somebody shouted. "There's the man that killed Poker."

Hagar turned to see that it was the cowpuncher with the bottle. A group of men two doors down began moving up toward him. They had all been drinking; their faces were flushed; their eyes excited. Over their heads, Hagar saw the hearse coming up the street. Little Al was on the high box seat with the driver.

Missouri saw it, too, and tried to pull Hagar into the doorway of the harness shop. But the knot of men broke around them, catching Hagar's arm, jostling him. The cowpuncher with the bottle reached them, handing it over the bobbing heads.

"Have a drink, Hagar. You deserve one. You deserve a dozen."

"Yeah," shouted another man. "He done the town a public service. We oughta throw a celebration for him. They're giving Poker a party . . . let's give Hagar a party!"

Hagar whirled, fighting to get free. But more men were joining the crowd, moving down toward the nearest saloon, and both he and Missouri were drawn helplessly with them. The band was nearing now. Its brazen clangor, the explosive thump of the great drum, the shrill squawk of the cracked cornet added to the din of shouting voices.

"This ain't no way to treat the hero of War Bonnet. You're knockin' him around like a cork. Up on the shoulders, up on the shoulders!"

The crowd took up the cry. Hands clawed at Hagar's elbows, his legs. Again he fought, but the overwhelming pressure of numbers finally caught him up. Lifted off the ground in their clawing hands, he heard Missouri's hoarse voice.

"Not up there, you fools! Little Al! Can't you see Little Al? Don't lift him up there."

But they paid no attention to Missouri. It was as if the sound bore Hagar upward. The cacophonous din deafened him, till the shouted words, the booming drum, the blaring brass became one vast wave of noise.

Lifted with his feet kicking higher than his head, he caught sight of the band. It was not fifty yards down the street, coming inexorably toward him. The swamper was first. He was whanging the triangle with methodical abandon, without regard to tempo or to what the other musicians were playing. Then the tuba player, his cheeks puffed out like red apples. And the cornet player, pointing his instrument to the sky. And the tall, skinny one beating at his bass drum with a rapt expression on his face, totally oblivious of the mob of kids running with him and trying to push the curly-headed boy from beneath the drum so they could carry it on their backs.

Then Hagar was seated on a pair of stout shoulders, rocking, jerking. Across the bobbing heads, the sweating faces, the tops of fifty hats, his eyes met Little Al's.

The huge saloon-keeper seemed to lift up on the seat of the hearse. His mouth opened, his eyes widened, a deep tension dug cavities in his face. For just that instant they stared at each other across the top of the crowd, with the noise so loud it was almost painful. Then Hagar's support seemed to collapse beneath him, and he was falling.

He did not go clear down. The press was too close for that. Caught in the pinch of bodies, he saw that one of the men who had been carrying him was down on his knees. He saw Missouri beside him, and knew he had pulled the man down.

Missouri caught at Hagar, elbowing and kicking to make

a place for him on the ground. Others started fighting back. The mob swirled around Hagar, knocking him this way and that. He lost contact with Missouri. An eddy of the struggling, shouting men swept him into the alley mouth. He broke free and stumbled into the slot between the buildings. He stopped against the wall, panting, his coat torn half off.

Then another man came into the alley, sliding around the corner, as if he had been up against the wall of the building along the boardwalk. It was Jack Willows.

Hagar elbowed his torn coat off the butt of his gun, calling hoarsely to the man. "Willows, if you make a move, I swear I'll shoot you! I'm fed up, I swear!"

"Don't be crazy," Willows said. He stopped, hands held wide, a crooked grin on his slack-jawed face. "I come peaceable, Hagar. You can't go out the front way, with Little Al waiting for you. Let's go on down to the back alley and talk."

"Missouri . . . ?"

"Last I saw, Missouri was heading toward the Pioneer House. Looked like he was leading them down that way so you could get free here." Willows shifted the inevitable plug from one leathery cheek to the other, snorting. "Funny, ain't it?"

"No," said Hagar.

The sly humor left Willows. "I didn't mean it that way. We all know you ain't afraid of Little Al. Not after whipping Drumgriffin and sitting it out with Poker that way. You're just fed up, like you say. You got nothing against Little Al, and you don't wanna have to kill him."

Hagar sagged tiredly against the weathered siding, still watching the man warily. "That's about it."

"Then why not come with me? Missouri's all right. He can take care of hisself. This'll only be a few minutes."

"What will?"

"Garland has a proposition for you. He's waiting up in Cimarron Alley," Willows said.

Hagar straightened a little against the wall, face tightening.

Willows moved tentatively toward him, grinning. "Take it easy. This is all above the board. You said you're fed up. This is your chance to get out. Five minutes and you're out."

A man came stumbling out of the crowd, holding his face, and went to his hands and knees in the alley. There was the splintering tinkle of a broken bottle. Hagar saw that the crowd had filled the street now, stopping the funeral procession. Over their heads he could see the black top of the hearse.

"Little Al's still out there," Willows said. "He saw you come in here."

Hagar stared at the man a moment, eyes slitted. "You go first," he said.

Chapter Sixteen

It took them ten minutes to reach Cimarron Alley, down the back alleys, the twisting cross lines that paralleled Center Street. At the bottom of the alley, where the first squalid shanties began, they stopped. Willows pointed up the slope.

"It's that cabin up near the end," he said. "Since you whipped Drumgriffin, the feeling in town has changed so much that it was safer for Garland to stay up here."

Hagar stopped beside a pair of grubby miner's children playing listlessly in the dooryard. "You kids seen a bunch of cowhands around here this morning?"

A curly-haired boy looked up at him with solemn eyes, shaking his head. "Just you, mister."

"Who lives up at the log cabin?"

"Two men."

"Nobody else has gone in there today?"

"Just him."

Hagar followed the boy's eyes back to Willows. The man was grinning thinly. "Don't you think everybody's learned they'd better play the game your way by now, Hagar?" he asked.

"Let's go," Hagar said.

A mangy dog followed them on up the rocky slope, sniffing at Hagar's boots. They halted before the log shack. Its upper end sank into the ground.

"Go on in," Willows said.

"You tell Garland to come out."

"Ed, I got him."

In a moment the door was shoved open, scraping against the puncheon floor. Garland had to stoop to get out. He was in his shirt sleeves, a freshly rolled smoke in one hand. The domineering grooves of his face spread into a humorless smile. "I thought maybe you'd be ready to deal."

"I'll talk business, when you bring the other man out."

Garland looked surprised, then grinned thinly. "I suppose you have a right to be suspicious." He half turned his head. "Pat, he won't talk till he's sure this isn't another trap. Come out."

There was a scrape of a chair, a wheezing breath. Boots dragged across the puncheons. Drumgriffin had to stoop to get through the door, too. He straightened slowly, blinking his eyes in the strong light.

The change in the man shocked Hagar. He seemed shrunken. He did not stand at his full height. His shoulders looked stooped, pinched together, robbing his great chest of all its depth. Some of the long scars on his cheeks had become infected and were covered with bruises. He was puffed up about one eye, about the lips. A two days' growth of greasy, blue beard covered his chin, and a little muscle kept twitching uncontrollably across his jaw. But it was the eyes that told the story more than anything else. One of them was purplish, still almost closed. The other was bloodshot, glazed, watering in the sunlight. They would not meet Hagar's glance for a long time. They lifted slowly from the ground, and, when they finally focused on Hagar, they held the sullen, furtive look of a cowed dog.

Then Drumgriffin looked down again, at the half-filled glass of whiskey in his hand. A guttural little sound ran through him, like the growl of some animal.

Garland smiled thinly. "I always wondered what would happen when Pat was really whipped. I always wondered if that pride could take it."

Drumgriffin's head jerked faintly toward Garland, and the words left him huskily. "Damn you, Ed, if you. . . ."

"Shut up, Pat," Garland snapped. He did not even look at Drumgriffin. "Now, Hagar," he said, "I'll come down to cases. I've got pride, too, and I had to swallow a lot of it to invite you up here like this. But you've hung onto that Quarter long enough to force my hand. I could have you killed, and wait for the land to revert to the government, and go through the formalities of having someone file on it again for me. But it would be out of my hands too long that way. The other factions would get too strong in Converse County, while I was waiting. I've got to have that land now, and I'm willing to pay for it."

He turned to pace the way he had when they first met, rubbing at the back of his neck. "I can't offer you cash. I guess you know that by now. I'm the richest man in Wyoming, but it's all beef or land or politicians or whatever I've had to buy to keep my machine going. Come fall beef shipment, I'll have cash again. Enough to buy War Bonnet, if I have to. I plan on dumping three thousand head. But right now the sack's empty. So here's the deal."

He turned and paced back toward Hagar. The cigarette was in his mouth now, and Willows stepped forward to light it. Garland halted his driven pacing to cup his hands around the match. He took a drag, glanced sharply at Hagar.

"I'll pay you in cattle. Your last price for the Quarter was ten thousand? I'll do better than that. Chicago's quoting ten dollars a hundred. That's forty dollars a head for your average steer. When I ship this fall, three hundred head will be yours. I'll give you a letter of credit now. After September First you can pick up the money at any Burnside packing office in the West."

Hagar was listening to him, but his eyes were on Drum-griffin. The man had stood through it all, hunched over, a drunken slackness to his stubbled jaw. Hagar could not believe that a mere physical whipping could break a man that way.

"That's twelve thousand dollars, Hagar," Garland was saying. "All you have to do for the extra two thousand is wait till Burnside has my cattle. The letter of credit is as good as money in the bank."

Hagar met his eyes. "Providing I cash it any place but in Laramie."

Garland smiled sardonically. "You get the idea. The farther away, the better. That's why I didn't offer you this kind of deal till I had to. If it got around that I paid you in cattle instead of cash, they'd know I was in a hole. There are a hundred coyotes just waiting to pull me down. If any of my creditors put the pressure on, I could pay all right. But I'd have to sell out somewhere along the line, and that would put a hole in the wall."

"And water through one hole can wash away the dam," Hagar said. "How does it feel to be riding a razor, Garland?"

"That's my business. It won't be for long. With the Quarter in my hands, Converse County will be mine. It'll tip the balance of power my way in the state. But what do you care? You'll be out of it."

"And you'll do this to Nicholet," Hagar said, still looking at the Irishman.

Garland frowned. "What?"

"You swore Nicholet would be first," Hagar said. "And then Cheryl. Cherington. Anybody who blocked you."

Garland suddenly understood. He glanced at Drum-griffin, smiling sardonically. "I didn't do that. You did."

"I was just an instrument," Hagar said. "You did it as surely as if you'd beaten him with your own hands. It wasn't the fight that broke him, Garland. It was the way you used him. Used his love for Cheryl, knowing what it would do to him, if he lost, in front of her. I'm glad he was here today, Garland. I'm glad I saw him like this."

"What are you talking about?" Drumgriffin flung the glass from him, trying to straighten up. "I ain't washed up. Cheryl ain't that kind of a woman. Just because you whipped me. . . ."

He started to lurch forward, but Garland caught him. "Damn you, Pat! Don't mess this up now."

Pain crossed the big Irishman's face as he struggled to free himself. His voice was slurred with drink. "Leggo, Garland! I ain't washed up!"

"Aren't you?" Garland's words left him in a vicious gust as he smashed an elbow into Drumgriffin's middle.

The Irishman's face contorted with pain. He doubled over, clawing at Garland to retain his feet. Garland tore loose and pulled his fist back to knock Drumgriffin away.

Hagar took a lunging step toward them, caught Garland's arm, and spun him around. Then he hit him in the face.

The blow knocked Garland back through the door. Hagar jumped after him. Staggering backward, Garland would have fallen, if he had not met the table. Hagar caught him there before he could regain his balance. Hagar hit him again.

Garland skidded bodily across the top of the table and flopped off on the other side, coming to a stop in a heap against the wall. Hagar wheeled back, knowing what Willows would do. The man had been forced to shove Drumgriffin out of the way, and that had held him up an instant. He was just coming through the door, pulling at his gun.

"You really want to?" Hagar said.

Willows stopped, with his hand on his gun. He looked at Hagar's hand, held over the butt of his Remington. Willows settled back, taking his hand off his gun. There was a sullen frustration working at his face.

Hagar turned so he could see Garland without putting Willows completely from his sight. The rancher had pulled himself to a sitting position. His face was smeared with blood. His breathing held a sobbing sound.

"I've wanted to do that for a long time," Hagar said.

"You bastard," Garland wheezed. "I'll kill you for that."

Hagar waited for him to get up. He didn't. Hagar wheeled, and walked out the door. Willows had to jump to get out of the way.

"If you try again, I'm not going to ask you," Hagar told Willows. "I'm going to pull, and I'm going to shoot your guts out. Unless you want that, just stand there and be good."

Drumgriffin was huddled against the wall, hugging his body. He looked at Hagar with squinted eyes glazed with pain, anger, confusion.

"Thanking you is a helluva thing," he said roughly.

"You don't have to," Hagar said. "That was for my own peace of mind. Looks like you got a couple of cracked ribs."

"In the fight," Drumgriffin said. "Don't you know how hard you hit?"

"And Garland knew they were cracked."

Drumgriffin spat. "I shouldn't even talk with you. I should want to take a gun to you."

"Do you?"

Drumgriffin straightened, still hugging himself. He took

165

a strained breath. The deep cavities of pain in his bruised face washed out a little. He stared at Hagar a long time. "No," he said at last. "Because I know it wouldn't do any good. Cheryl's yours. Killing you wouldn't change anything."

Hagar studied the man's face. "Is that true, Drumgriffin?"

"It's always been true. She was never in love with me. She might have thought she was. She might have convinced herself I was what she wanted, because I was solid. I'd settled down. I had big dreams. But I saw the change in her the minute you hit town. And then I saw her yesterday. She had great pity for me. That's all she had."

Hagar looked at the ground. "That can take the guts out of a man."

"It can . . . when she was all he wanted in the world. Don't wait until it's too late, Hagar. That's why I lost her. She's got to know where a man stands. I didn't make my stand soon enough. She was right. I should have pulled out from Garland a long time ago, no matter what the cost. She saw what it would do to me, if I didn't."

Hagar was frowning deeply. "Nicholet told me the same thing. He said perhaps Cheryl saw the thing more clearly than we did."

"Are you applying it to yourself, Hagar?" Drumgriffin said.

Hagar looked up sharply. There was no anger, no pain left in Drumgriffin's eyes. They were clear and waiting.

"I'll help you down to the doctor's," Hagar said abruptly. "You better get those ribs taped up."

Chapter Seventeen

By three in the afternoon the funeral was over, the musicians were back in front of Little Al's, playing their lungs out, and the streets were full of riotous crowds. Hagar gained the Pioneer House by the back alleys, after leaving Drumgriffin at the doctor's. He didn't want to be dragged into the mob again by drunken men who wanted to fête a hero.

He went into the rear door of the Pioneer House and through to the bar. Missouri was standing at its front end, nervously twirling a drink. Relief lit his long face at sight of Hagar.

"What in hell happened to you? I combed the town, after I led that crowd away. I thought you'd come up here."

Hagar stopped beside him. It had been no more than half an hour since he had seen Missouri, but it seemed like much longer. "I've just seen something that took the bottom out of my belly," he said.

Missouri slid him the drink. "I haven't touched it yet." His eyes squinted with sly speculation as Hagar tossed it off neat. "Drumgriffin?" he asked.

Hagar put the empty glass down. "How did you know?"

"I thought it was about time for Garland to make his last offer," Missouri said. "You messed up Drumgriffin pretty bad, didn't you?"

"He's a broken man, Missouri. It's not nice to think I had a hand in it."

"He could have taken the physical beating," Missouri said. "Maybe he could even have stood up under losing

167

Cheryl. But the two of them combined knocked the props from under him."

Hagar shook his head. "Garland made a mistake in letting me see Drumgriffin. I realized that's what Garland would do to you, to Nicholet, to Cheryl, to every one of my friends in this town, if he got hold of the Quarter."

"That only leaves the ranchers," Missouri said. "Why don't we go to the meeting? Garland must be pretty close to the wall, if he actually tried to make a deal with you. It might give the ranchers the confidence they need."

"I told you I'd close today, didn't I?" Hagar said. He stared at the empty glass, only dimly feeling the subtle change that seeing Drumgriffin had produced in him. "Let's go," he said.

They turned out through the lobby together. Hagar let Missouri go through the front door first, then started to follow. But Missouri blocked him, backing in again.

"Paul," he said. "You go around the back way. I'll get the horses and pick you up there."

Past Missouri, over the heads of the men still milling around in the street, Hagar could see Little Al in front of his saloon, talking with Tanglefoot.

"Damn it," he said.

Missouri turned to Hagar. "Paul, we know you aren't afraid of him."

"You don't have to give me a sales talk, Missouri," Hagar said heavily. "I told you I was fed up. There's no reason for this, and I'm not going to make one. I'll meet you out back."

He went through the lobby and the bar into the hall leading to the rear door. He waited there till Missouri rode around, leading his horse. They left town by the back alleys, breaking into a trot on the road. For a time the banks on either side were purple with blooming asters. The mountains rose in timber-blanketed walls, steeped with a pungency of pine and the musty smell of drying grass. They crossed a chuckling stream whose quiet pools were broken by the splash of black-spotted trout, and then climbed through a cañon choked with firs girdled by white, gummy bands where porcupines had gnawed off the bark. Finally the mountains opened up and left sun-drenched parks where cattle grazed in peace.

Missouri had been watching Hagar's attention to the scene, and at last he spoke. "It's a good country, Paul. You'd travel all your life and not find a better one."

"With Little Al waiting to dust me off every time I poke my nose out?"

"He'll cool down."

Hagar shifted restlessly in the saddle, turned moody by the half-defined things stirring within him. He was remembering what Drumgriffin had said. He couldn't believe the man was right. Cheryl had said herself that merely whipping a man in the street would not gain her love. If she was through with Drumgriffin, why hadn't she shown it somehow? Why that reserve at the bar before the inquest? These things kept pulling at Hagar, turning him morose, and something else, working deeper, something he could not even define, filled him with an intense restlessness.

It took them two hours to reach Cherington's place. The valley opened out into the flats, and they left the War Bonnet Road and took a cutoff that led them into a fold of hills on the west side of the valley. Here the shadows were long and cool, dropping over the white frame house, the outbuildings, the snake fence that meandered peacefully down the side of the road.

They pulled through the gate, seeing about a dozen men

gathered among the buggies, the wagons, the horses in the dooryard.

Cherington broke free of the group to greet them. "Didn't expect you, Hagar," he said in pleased surprise. "It might help a lot. Light down and meet the boys. You know Karatt. This here is Glen Alder . . . owns the Lucky Seven. Charlie Davis . . . R Over R."

Alder was tall and stooped with haggard lines in his thin face. Davis was shorter, beefier, with curly red hair and a freckled, snub nose. Hagar shook hands with them, seeing the reserved speculation in their eyes. Cherington was about to introduce another man when a pair of riders turned in from behind the poplars at the gate. The friendly talk died as one by one the men turned to look. It was Nicholet on his big white mare, and Muley Banning. Hagar saw anger dig its furrows around Cherington's compressed lips.

"I thought you wasn't coming, Muley."

Nicholet reined his mare in. "I cooled him off, Bob. Convinced him he should give this thing a chance. He's the biggest one of the bunch . . . next to you . . . and we haven't rightly got a chance without him."

Cherington frowned, then said reluctantly: "All right. I suppose we might as well get started." He moved through the crowd to the steps, where he could be seen by all. "Here it is, the way Nicholet gave it to me last night. Hagar wants ten thousand. We put up our twenty-five hundred, as agreed. Nicholet offers to loan us the balance."

"Muley told me the interest was twenty per cent," Alder said. "How could we ever pay it back at those rates?"

Cherington turned on Banning, face growing ruddy with anger. "You told him that?"

"Not exactly." Banning swung off his horse to stand among the men. "I know Nicholet's charged that before on short-term loans. I just said I didn't believe a man who worked that way would hand us over seventy-five hundred for nothing."

"It isn't for nothing," Cherington said. "You're just trying to twist this up. Any fool can see the stake Nicholet has in this."

As Cherington went on, Hagar moved to Nicholet, asking him: "Why did you bring Banning? You knew this would happen."

"I hoped it wouldn't." The lawyer's frown was worried. "Banning promised me. . . ."

"Did you bring the contract?" Banning shouted.

The lawyer looked up in surprise, then recovered himself. "Yes. Of course. You can all see it."

From his inside pocket he brought a sheaf of manila-backed paper and handed it over to Banning. They passed it among themselves, frowning over it, some of them working their lips soundlessly as they read.

Banning objected disgustedly. "It's just what I thought. One of them damned legal papers so complicated you can't make head or tail of it. How'd we know what we're signing?"

Hagar strode among them, taking the paper from Karatt. He read through it, frowning over the obscure clauses, the legal terminology. "Did you have to make it up like this?" he asked the lawyer. "It's a simple deal."

"On the contrary," Nicholet said. "There are a dozen men representing the party of the first part. There are too many things that simply have to be included to make it a valid instrument."

"But you know they can't understand this."

"I can explain each clause to them."

"You could make black look like white, if they gave you

enough words," Banning said. "I've signed too many papers without knowing what was in them."

"Banning," Cherington said hoarsely, "you're twisting this all around again, just like you did before."

"I'm not twisting anything," Banning said, his voice lifting. "I'm just not staking my whole future on a deal like this."

"That's right," Alder said. "My outfit's mortgaged to the hilt now."

"You're not mortgaging anything," Cherington said. His fists were clenched with repressed anger. "It's just a simple note."

"Nothing simple about it," Banning said.

"Damn it, Banning, will you shut up?"

"I will not. I got as much voice in this as you have, Cherington."

"Not when you try to bust it apart. If you hadn't come tonight, we could have made these men see the light."

"Then I'm glad I came. I don't want to see my friends sucked in on something where they lose their shirts. I'm not signing this paper. Are you, Karatt?"

The man shook his cropped head. "I can't understand what it says at all."

"How'd we ever pay him back?" Alder called. "I don't think I've made seventy-five hundred dollars in all my life."

"And you won't have to make it for the rest of your life to pay this debt," Hagar said angrily. "It isn't a matter of one man owing all that money. There's a dozen of you here. It will be spread over a period of ten years, according to the contract. That's only about seventy dollars a year for each of you. If you'd ever stop thinking of yourselves just once, and think of the group. . . ."

He broke off, surprised he had gone so far. Something

about their squabbling voices, their blind objections had angered him. But they were all turned toward him now.

"What right you got to butt in?" Banning asked roughly.

"It's my land you're arguing about, isn't it?" Hagar said. "But it won't matter whose land it is, if you don't use your heads. Somebody closes that pass off for just one season, and you'll all be wiped out in a die-up. You're so divided now, any move Garland made could ruin you. If you stood together, he couldn't. He's got his back to the wall."

"How do you know?" Karatt asked.

"He just offered me cattle for the Bloody Quarter."

Alder frowned. "He hasn't got the cash?"

"Not a cent. He's been climbing so fast he hasn't had a chance to consolidate. He's got as many holes in his machine as you have. If he doesn't get the pass, he won't be the big man in the state any more. You could keep him from getting it."

He saw the stir this caused among them, but Banning stopped it with his hasty shout: "I ain't signing any contract."

"Then don't sign, damn you," Hagar said. "What if you didn't have to? What if you had the pass in your hands, right now?"

"You're talking crazy," Karatt said.

"I'm asking you a simple question. If you had that pass, would you stand together, would you drive through with Cherington?"

"I was willing to do it before," Karatt said.

"Would you?" Hagar asked Alder.

"I would, if Davis would."

"I would," Davis said.

"What are we trying to pull?" Banning asked angrily.

Hagar stared around at the circle, seeing the strength in

their faces, strength that would let them stand against any odds, if they could only join their forces. And he knew what had been working at him on the way here. It wasn't merely their squabbling and blindness that had caused this. That had only brought to a head what must have been forming within him for days. It let him see his path clearly for the first time.

"It's obvious you aren't going to buy the pass. And I won't sell to Garland. All that leaves is for me to keep it myself. But I'm not going to do it for nothing. If you prove to me you've got the guts to stick together . . . to buck Garland . . . I'll guarantee you free passage through the pass as long as I own it."

Banning shouted: "A speculator like you doesn't change overnight. How could we trust you?"

Missouri stepped in beside Hagar. "If he gives his word, I'll stand behind him."

"You're the railroad man," Karatt said.

"He's the railroad man," Alder said. It went around among them like that, an excited buzzing of words, of how Missouri had been here for months, working under cover, of how he had revealed himself at the coroner's inquest. And now Hagar knew why Missouri had shown his true colors. "You damned old fox," he told him.

"Does that mean the railroad will stand behind him?" Karatt asked.

Missouri was grinning. "It does."

Karatt turned to Alder, speaking in a hurried voice. "They wouldn't back anybody they weren't sure of."

Alder scratched his neck. "I don't know. His word must be plenty good, if the whole railroad will stand behind it."

Then a woman came out onto the porch, a calico apron over her wine-colored dress, and moved down through the crowd, the soft lights from the house catching up little flecks of gold in her hair. She stopped beside Hagar, smiling at him.

"Cheryl," he breathed in whispered surprise.

"I came out to help Missus Cherington serve," she said. Then she turned to the men. "I've loaned you money. I've bunked you, when you couldn't pay me. I've put you to bed drunk. I've made clothes for those of you who aren't married. Have you ever known me to tell a lie?"

"No, Cheryl," Karatt said. "My Lord. . . ."

"Then let me tell you this. I've known Paul Hagar most of my life. If he says he'll stick, he'll stick."

There was a moment of silence. Then Karatt said in a loud voice: "That's enough for me. If the railroad and Cheryl Bannister stand behind him, he's got to be right."

"You damn' fools!" Banning said. "This is worse than ever. How do you know Hagar hasn't made a deal with Garland?"

"The arguing is through," Hagar said. "If you aren't with us, you can leave."

"I ain't leaving until I've had my say!"

"You're through saying. You've twisted it around long enough. Are you getting out, or am I putting you out?"

Hagar took a step toward the man as he said it, putting him a foot from Banning. The rancher's sloping shoulders settled. The lines of his weathered face carved themselves deeper.

"Damn you!" he said. "You couldn't put me out."

"Be careful, Muley," Karatt said. "You saw what he did to Drumgriffin."

For a moment longer Banning faced him. There was not a sound. The smell of sun-heated dust hung bitterly in the air. Then Banning let out his breath. It was guttural with animal rage. "You'll be sorry you got sucked into this. Sooner than you think."

He wheeled and stomped to his dun, swinging up with that whipping motion Hagar had seen before. He jerked the horse around brutally and put the spurs to it. The beast whinnied shrilly and bolted. Cherington watched him ride out of the yard, then turned gravely to Hagar.

"When do we start?"

"We'd better start right now," Hagar said. "You all got your cattle gathered?"

"Mine are still below the pass," Cherington said. "The rest of the men have theirs on their own holding ground. They've been waiting to see what was going to be done."

"You can all make it to the pass in one night, if you push. That would leave you ready to start through at dawn."

"Give us an hour for grub? Missus Cherington was planning on it."

"You've got it."

They all gathered around, talking, congratulating Hagar, asking him a flood of questions, but finally Cherington got them herded into the house. Missouri gave Hagar a knowing grin and trailed along. Hagar was left alone with Cheryl. In the gathering dusk her face was turned up to him, eyes shining softly.

"Is that what you wanted?" he asked soberly.

"It's what I wanted, Paul," she said. "But it's what you wanted, too. That's why I kept out of it. If it was going to happen, I wanted you to do the whole thing yourself. I'd prodded you into that livery-stable deal, when you didn't really want it. I prodded you into that general store, even put up the money, trying to force you into a mold you weren't ready to accept. If I had shown myself before the last moment tonight, I wouldn't really have known whether you did it for me or for yourself. They say we often speak the truth in anger. The men made you angry. You reacted with what you really felt. It brought out what you truly wanted to do."

"Why didn't you tell me all this in the hotel . . . after my fight with Drumgriffin?" he asked.

"You weren't ready, Paul. All you offered me was a kiss, then." She held his eyes a moment, but at last her head bowed. "I suppose I was really fighting my love for you, too. I didn't want it to look like merely whipping Pat would change me. Because it wouldn't. I was changing long before the fight . . . without realizing it."

He smiled softly. "At this point I would have kissed you, in Denver."

"You were never a man to hesitate," she said.

The passion of it was not lessened. It swept him as intensely as before, giving him an almost painfully acute consciousness of her ripe body straining against him. But there was something more. When she finally drew her lips away and put her cheek against his chest, he was filled with a sense of fulfillment that had been completely lacking in the hotel room. With her face pressed to his chest, her eyes closed, she spoke in a soft whisper.

"War Bonnet is going to be much better than Denver," she said. "Much, much better than Denver."

Chapter Eighteen

Hagar had no more time with Cheryl that night. Right after eating, they started for the pass. Cheryl insisted so ardently on joining them that they allowed her to go as far as Cherington's bed grounds below the pass, on the condition that she stay there with the cook when the drive started. They were all sure that Garland would try to stop them, and there would be fighting. Their only hope was that they could get the combined herd through the pass before Garland could gain more help from Laramie. All he had now was his E Bar G crew, and, while they outnumbered the ranchers, they were far less dangerous alone than they would be joined to a herd of gunslicks dredged up from the southern town.

Half the War Bonnet cattlemen were so small that they ran no crews at all. Banning was the biggest, with four men, and his loss cut a hole in their numbers. It was Hagar's idea to send as many men as possible up on the ridge on either side of the pass. Garland could not approach from any direction without running into one of them or, at least, being seen, and they would have warning of his presence long before he reached the herd.

One by one, as the outfits straggled in, joining their cattle to those already on the holding ground, Hagar picked his men from among the operators and crews and sent them to their positions above the pass. Long before dawn, the number he had been allotted was used up. Then there was the wait, with the outfits still arriving, the dusty men gathering around the fires, sipping at their coffee, talking in ner-

178

vous, little gusts. Then, near dawn, they began to drift toward the cattle. Hagar and Cheryl had their moment by the fire, when they were able to express what they really felt as they could not before the men.

"When will I know?"

"As soon as the herd is through the pass, they'll be safe," he said. "I'll be back then. Noon, maybe."

She seemed to lift toward him. "Paul. . . ."

"Cheryl. . . ."

She subsided, eyes dropping. "I won't act like a woman. Just come back to me, Paul."

"I will, Cheryl. Nothing in this world can stop me."

A sun-flushed sky backlighted somber hogbacks by the time Missouri and Hagar reached the heights above the pass, riding the line of flankers they had sent out. Far below, the herd started up toward the pass, pressed into a snake-like column as soon as it moved into the jaws of the mountains. Riding up through the stands of spruce, through the studding of boulders hoary with buckwheat, through the birch brush stippled with crimson buffalo berries, Hagar shivered in the early morning chill. Missouri was busy lighting a cigar.

"Good land over this east ridge," he said. "I understand some dry-land farmer homesteaded this piece and then couldn't make a go of it. You could probably get it from him at two bits an acre."

"You can give up that sales talk now," Hagar grinned.

"I was just pointing things out. I promised you a deal with the railroad. With the money you get from them, you could buy a sizable bunch of brood stock."

"Is that Finley up ahead?"

Missouri's head lifted. He squinted his eyes against the silver dawn, then nodded. They scrambled their horses up a long talus slope onto a wind-swept ridge of exposed granite, where one of Cherington's riders was standing beside his horse.

"Nothing yet," he said. "I run out of makings."

Hagar tossed down a sack of tobacco and his book of cigarette papers. "How long ago did you leave Bruce?"

"Twenty minutes. Not a bobble from him."

The man rolled a cigarette and handed back the makings. Hagar and Missouri left him, dropping off the rocky ridge into a saddle. They passed Bruce and another man farther on. The cattle toiled along through the pass below, almost hidden in the buttery haze of dust they were stirring up. Half a mile ahead, Hagar saw the beginning of the chasm. Some ancient upheaval had cracked the floor of the pass, leaving a deep gorge that twisted and turned along the western flank. The eastern side was a narrow plateau that paralleled the crack, its wall dropping off a hundred feet into the chasm.

"That's our weak point," Missouri said. "Spook them cattle anywhere along there and they'll stampede over that edge. It would finish us for good."

"I've planted the men closer here," Hagar said. "Garland won't be able to get through without some shooting. It should warn us in plenty of time."

But a brooding somberness settled into Hagar's face as he began to realize for the first time what a responsibility he had shouldered, promising these men passage through his land. Today would either make or break them all.

They began to climb out of the gorge, through stunted juniper and dwarf cedar. They came to the base of a talus slope, too steep and treacherous for a horse. Hagar stared down the fringe of dwarf timber that stopped at this point.

"Didn't Davis have his horse hitched here?"

Missouri met Hagar's eyes. Then, without speaking, they both dismounted. It was a scramble to get up the talus slope. Missouri slipped once and almost slid back down. Then they were above it, moving through exposed bedrock to the peak. They found the short, red-headed man in a little cove of rock, where he had taken up his station, sprawled flat on his face. Both men crouched over him, the wind whipping softly at the hat brims.

"Looks like somebody whacked him on the head," Missouri said. "He's still breathing."

Their eyes met. "How could they reach him?" Hagar wondered. "Nobody could get within a hundred yards of this place without being seen."

Missouri frowned. "There's really only one possibility. He wouldn't let anybody come that near unless he knew him and trusted him."

"That's about it," Hagar said bitterly. "Maybe Banning?"

Hagar stood up so that he could see down into the pass. The cattle were curling around the approach to the plateau that paralleled the chasm.

"Looks like Garland probably got through," Hagar speculated.

"If he did, it wasn't your fault," Missouri assured him. "You didn't count on a stab in the back like this."

"It's obvious they mean to jump that herd when it reaches the chasm," Hagar said. "We've got to get down there."

"We can't leave Davis."

"We've got to. There's no time. He'll come out of just a bang on the head all right."

Reluctantly they left the man, scrambling down to their horses. It was a wild ride, with the horses fighting to keep their feet, plunging down till they reached heavier timber.

The lodgepoles shot a hundred feet into the sky. The slanting shafts of morning sunlight turned the lanes between the trees into gigantic cathedral aisles.

They reached an open park and lunged across, dodging boulders. A picket-pin squirrel ran chattering before them and spooked the horses. Fighting his frightened animal, Hagar hit the edge of the park and plunged into a dense stand of timber. He almost ran into the E Bar G horse hitched to some buckbrush.

His horse veered wildly, lost its footing, and went down. He kicked free and hit hard, rolling, with a dim sense of Jack Willows jumping up from behind a fallen log and firing at him. A bullet slashed into pine needles a foot behind Hagar's rolling body. It made him keep rolling till he had his gun out, and then he stopped and shot Willows.

Missouri came lunging in from the park in time to see it. He fought his horse to a dancing, pirouetting stop. Hagar realized that Willows's horse had torn free of its tie and was running off down through the timber, accompanied by his own animal.

"Get on down to Cherington!" Hagar shouted. "You've got to reach him before Garland makes his bid. Put those cattle in a mill. It's the only way to stop them from stampeding, if Garland gets through."

"What about you?"

"My horse is gone. I'll do what I can to stop it up here."

"But I can't leave you."

"Dammit, Missouri, you're the only one who can reach them in time."

Missouri gave him a tortured look, then put spurs to his horse. "I'll be back with men, Paul."

As Carnes plunged on down through the trees, Hagar ran over to Willows. The man had dragged himself to a sitting position against the log, holding a bloody thigh with both hands.

"Where's Garland?"

"The hell with you."

Hagar bent down and bunched the man's shirt front in his fist. "I've never hit a wounded man before."

Willows pulled back from the savage expression in Hagar's face. Perhaps he was remembering Drumgriffin. "Damn you," he said. "Down in that draw to the north. He put me up here as lookout. I was supposed to signal when the cattle got opposite that drop-off. You'll never stop him alone."

But Hagar had already left him, scooping up the Winchester Willows had dropped, running heavily downslope. The slope began to pitch off northward, and then, through the timber, he could see the draw. Garland had been holding his whole bunch at the box end of the narrow cut, but the shots between Willows and Hagar must have set them off. They were all swinging into their saddles, milling around, and shouting.

Down in the pass, Hagar could see the herd. Missouri had reached the men in the lead, but they hadn't started to mill the cattle yet. They would have to turn the cattle slowly or start a stampede themselves. Garland could still run the beef off the drop-off, if he struck now. There was only one way to stop him.

Hagar knew that if he could break their charge just once, Cherington would have time to mill the cattle. But it couldn't be done from up here on the flank. It would have to be from the front, and he'd have to take them by surprise—if they didn't know how many men were facing them. If he could knock enough of them out before they reached him, he might break their rush.

He had never stopped running, paralleling the edge of the draw, using timber to cover himself. He saw Garland break free of the press on a black with four white stockings. The man threw up his arm and shouted something, and the whole bunch broke into a gallop down the draw.

High on the bank above, Hagar reached the mouth of the draw at the same time. Still hoping to surprise them, he kicked off, sliding down through the brush, dodging a boulder, stooped low. But one of the Garland riders spotted him and began firing. He hit bottom with bullets biting into the earth all around him. A boulder jutted into the draw from the bank, and he took refuge behind this.

They were still a hundred yards away, but the earth was trembling beneath him, and it looked like a thousand horsemen pouring out of that narrow draw.

He opened fire at Garland. In the dust, he had no accuracy. He must have hit the black horse instead of Garland, for on his second shot the animal went down. His third shot emptied a man out of the saddle. They seemed right on top of him, burgeoning out of their own boiling dust.

Then a crackle of shots came from behind him, and he stared over his shoulder. Muley Banning was coming in from the pass with his four men. Hagar could not help whirling, a trapped feeling gagging him. The ground shook with Garland's men right behind him. Banning was only a hundred feet away, charging down on him. He raised his rifle.

Then he saw that there were other men with Banning—a Cherington rider, Alder, Missouri Carnes. He stared at them, still coming down on him, unable to believe it. But Missouri's grinning face finally convinced him. All of them were firing over his head at Garland's men. He wheeled back to see that the rush had been stopped.

The Garland riders were milling around in a curtain of white dust, horses rearing and squealing. A man broke from the mass toward Hagar, reeling over his saddle horn, and finally pitched off to hit the ground ten feet in front of the boulder. The horse ran on by, whinnying shrilly. Hagar added his fire to the din and saw another man go down.

Banning and his men pulled their horses up around Hagar, emptying their guns into the disorganized Garland riders. This broke them completely, and they scattered back into the draw in little bunches.

Missouri swung off his horse by Hagar. "You damn' fool, trying to stop the whole bunch by yourself!"

"What about Banning?" Hagar said.

"Looks like we figured him wrong."

"I couldn't sit on my hands any longer," Banning said. "You're a bunch of damn' fools, but I guess I'm a damn' fool, too."

"They're going to try again," Hagar said. "Get your men off their horses and spread them through the cover here."

The Garland men were rallying back in the draw, but Hagar could not see Garland himself. Then a Cherington rider appeared in the timber above. He was one of the men they had placed on the ridge as a flanker. Hagar knew they would all be coming in, drawn by the fire. With their added force they could stop the Garland men cold.

"They're coming," Missouri shouted.

Again the earth began to shake. Again it was the horses, the men burgeoning out of their own boiling dust. Hagar worked the Winchester till it was empty. The Garland riders came right up to the muzzles of their guns before they broke. Then, in the din, in the dust, in the whirl of screaming horses and roaring men and crashing guns, Hagar caught sight of four shadowy riders, farther back in the draw, scrambling up for timber.

At first he thought they were escaping. Then it struck him that they might mean to bypass this draw and strike the herd from the timber while the fight was occupying attention here. He cast one glance at Banning, at Missouri, sprawled out behind the rocks and in the cover of scrub timber. He was sure they could hold the Garland riders now. And he couldn't take a chance on those four going into the timber.

He left the cover of his boulder and ran out of the mouth of the draw. There was no time to reload his Winchester. He pulled his Remington, following the toes of the slope. They would have to come down this way again to reach the cattle, either off the slope or from a draw farther south.

Off to his right, in another curtain of dust, Hagar could see the cattle being turned into a mill. Then he caught sight of movement through the timber above him. It was the four horsemen, moving toward a narrow gully that opened into the pass ahead of him.

Hagar turned up into timber, wanting to reach them before they broke into the open above the gully. He'd have to get close for any accuracy with a six-gun, and he needed cover for that. He dodged through the trees, the chokecherry thickets, heading upward at an angle that would intersect their line of direction at the edge of timber overlooking the gully. They were so intent on gaining the gully that they did not see his approach. He was within a hundred feet of them, when the first rider lunged into the open, spurring his horse over the brink to slide down the steep bank. It was Garland.

As his horse plunged over the side, Garland must have caught sight of Hagar, coming at a run. The rancher twisted in the saddle and opened fire. Hagar's gun bucked in his hand, but it was still a long shot for a revolver.

The gunfire spooked Garland's horse. It reared, trying to turn on the slope, and spilled. Garland pitched out of the saddle.

The other riders plunged from the trees, shooting at Hagar. But he had been so intent on Garland that he reached the brink of the draw before he realized it. Whirling to fire at the other men, he stumbled over the edge and pitched off.

He tried to catch himself, couldn't, and flopped and slid all the way to the bottom. He came to a stop behind a turn in the gully, but when he rolled over and scrambled to his feet, it brought him out from behind the shoulder of the turn and into sight of Garland.

The man was just coming to his feet, pulling his holstered gun. Rage, hatred, vindication all dug the creases of his face deep as he brought the weapon up in a whipping draw. Their guns smashed simultaneously.

Hagar felt a great blow in his left arm. It tore him completely around and pitched him down on his face with stunning force. It was not conscious thought that made him roll back over, pawing for his gun on the ground. It was the reaction of years running down its time-worn path.

Then Hagar stopped, gun in hand, lying on his belly. Garland was on his back twenty feet from Hagar. He was looking at the sky with empty eyes. There was only a faint bewilderment in his face. It struck Hagar how much he looked like Carter John, in that glade down by Big Squaw Creek.

Half hidden from the men above by the shoulder of the gully, by the thick mat of brush in which he lay, Hagar waited tensely for them to plunge down on him. He had felt no pain in his left arm in that first moment of shock. Now it swept over him blindingly, sickeningly. He heard the snort of horses, the rattle of shale.

Then he realized how subdued the sounds were. As if the men had halted their animals on the brink, were holding them there. He realized that they could see Garland without seeing him, for Garland was around that turn.

"He's dead." It was one of the 'punchers. His voice sounded hollow, far away. "Garland's dead."

There was a pause, another stirring of shale. "Shall we go down?"

"What for?"

The voice had an empty, final sound. Hagar could almost see the loss in their faces, the defeat. Without Garland, it would do them no good to turn the cattle, to do anything. There was another rustling of shale, a snorting of horses, fading away slowly upslope.

Hagar was swept with a wave of nausea. He crawled to the bank, twisted around, sat up. He tried to rise, but he was too weak, and fell back in a sitting position against the bank. The shots from the other draw were sporadic, dying. Something was happening to his vision. Everything was fuzzy. When he saw the man coming toward him, he tried to react, but couldn't. Then surprise came dully to him. It was Nicholet.

"You've left your gun out in the draw," the lawyer said.

Hagar looked stupidly at his weapon, five feet from him. Then he tried to focus his eyes on Nicholet. "How'd you get here?"

"I tried to keep Banning from coming today."

"But he's all right. He's not with Garland."

"That's why I needed to keep him from coming. It was his men that turned the tide. I thought maybe he'd break up the meeting yesterday. That's why I brought him. But you prevented that."

Hagar shook his head feebly. There was something wrong with what Nicholet was saying. Why couldn't he concentrate?

"You must have the deed on your person, Hagar. You went out to Cherington's yesterday, meaning to sell. Maybe you even kept the quit-claim. All you'd have to do then is give it to whoever bought, and he could fill in the names."

Hagar frowned stupidly at the man. "How do you know about the quit-claim?"

"I drew it up for Poker. That's why he left the party of the second part blank. My name was going in there."

"You?"

"You don't think we'd let a fool like Russian Poker really head the War Bonnet Syndicate, do you?" Nicholet asked. "He was a good, colorful front. It left me free to play all ends against the middle."

Swept with an unreasonable anger, as he finally saw it, Hagar lunged away from the side of the gully. Nicholet's hand flashed to his coat and came out with his gun. Hagar could not have made it anyway. He fell back against the earth, sickened by the violent effort, clutching at his wounded arm. For the first time he realized how much blood he had lost. His sleeve was soaked. That was why he felt so weak. He opened his eyes again, breathing shallowly.

"You killed Carter John," he said dully.

Nicholet's smile was bland as ever. "By a process of elimination, we had long ago decided Carter John was the only man Garland could send in to file on the Quarter. When we heard that Garland had stirred up new trouble in the boundary squabble, keeping the land commissioner in Cheyenne longer than he'd planned, we became suspicious. Everything hinged on stopping whoever Garland sent to file. I couldn't trust such an important job to Poker's stupid saloon toughs. I began watching the south road myself. You came along right after I'd killed Carter John. That prevented me from taking a direct route back to War Bonnet. By the time I'd reached town, the Land Office was closed, and I couldn't find the clerk."

"And it was you that tried to bushwhack us on Cotton Creek," Hagar said thinly.

"That was my mistake. I assumed you'd have the deed on you, when you went for Poker's bid that day."

"And you'd never really intended to help the ranchers buy the Quarter."

"That was only bait. All my moves were designed to get you alone with the papers on you. But life had made such a wary man of you, Hagar."

"And we thought Banning got Davis," Hagar said bitterly.

"Up on the ridge?" Nicholet made a small smile. "I didn't want the cattle to get through any more than Garland did. I followed Garland and his riders out . . . waited till I saw where they were going to try to get through, then cut ahead of them. Davis let me come up to his spot without suspicion. Garland never knew who knocked Davis on the head, but he didn't have time to question."

"But why, Nicholet?" Hagar asked helplessly. "Why?"

Hagar had seen the same milky opacity come into the man's eyes when he had shot Garland's hat off in the street. "Do you think I want to be a two-bit shyster all my life? That's what Banning called me, wasn't it? You were willing to risk your life for ten thousand dollars. What do you think I'd risk to be the biggest man in Wyoming? Not just a tinhorn lawyer, not just the guiding light of a small-time gambling ring. Bigger than Garland ever dreamed of being. Hagar, I'd have smashed him in the dust . . . I'd have risen higher. . . ."

He broke off. A faint film of sweat shone on his face. He made a rueful little sound, staring down at Hagar. The blank look settled back into his mild features.

"Never mind. There will be two bullets in you, when they find you. They will think both of them came from Garland's gun. Do you wish to give me the papers now, or shall I get them afterward?"

Hagar stared into the milky eyes. A new anger swept him. He tried to lunge up. He saw the gun jerk.

But the booming shot came from somewhere else. Nicholet's face went blank with shock. Then pain twisted it, and he fell over backward. Hagar sank back against the side of the gully again, staring at the dead lawyer. Then he looked across the gully to the opposite bank. Little Al stood there.

"I heard he'd left town," the man said thickly. "I thought he'd be coming up here."

There was a great emptiness in Hagar. The capacity for emotion seemed to have been drained from him. "I thought it was me you were after," he said.

"Hell, no," Al said. His voice was husky and sharp-edged. "Nicholet sent Poker up to your shack to get those papers. He knew Poker wouldn't let it go without playing the game. And he knew you'd have to play it out till one of you got it. Fifty-fifty odds, but it was just as good as killing Poker."

There was a rattle of brush from down in the gully. Hagar realized the shooting had stopped. That was the only sound, that brush popping before the passage of someone, before the passage of Cheryl Bannister, as she came into sight, calling his name. Cherington came waddling through the thickets far behind her.

"We couldn't hold her back, dammit," he shouted. "She

heard the fighting and came right into it. I never thought a chuck wagon could make it up this pass."

Cheryl dropped to her knees beside Hagar, intense compassion shining in her eyes. "Missouri said you'd come over this way. We heard the shots."

She broke off as she recognized Nicholet, and Hagar saw the shock mingle with her compassion. Cherington pushed in, with Missouri behind him. The lean railroad man stopped above Hagar and gave a critical glance at his wound.

"If you tie something above that hole to stop the blood, you'll be a new man tomorrow," he said. Then he looked at Nicholet. "The fourth party?"

"That's about it," Hagar said feebly.

Missouri untied his handkerchief and stooped to make a tourniquet around Hagar's arm. "Let's get Paul out of here. It smells like a morgue."

They helped him to his feet, and he stumbled along between them down through the brush and out of the gully. Hagar saw that the cattle were safe. The fight was over. Another wave of nausea swept him, and he sagged heavily against Cheryl.

"Paul!" she exclaimed. "Paul, your arm!"

"That's all right," he told her. "I can still hold you with the other one."

He was sick and dizzy, but it did not stop the sense of peace, of great contentment growing in him. He suddenly realized, fully, what he had won. The passage of his feet made a gritty sound in the earth of his own land, and his woman was so close that her scent seemed to envelop him, and the world was turned to spring around him.